Edward Ledwich Mitford

The Arab's Pledge

A Tale of Marocco in 1830

Edward Ledwich Mitford

The Arab's Pledge
A Tale of Marocco in 1830

ISBN/EAN: 9783744749602

Printed in Europe, USA, Canada, Australia, Japan

Cover: Foto ©Andreas Hilbeck / pixelio.de

More available books at **www.hansebooks.com**

THE ARAB'S PLEDGE:

A TALE OF MAROCCO

IN

1830.

BY

EDWARD L. MITFORD,

CEYLON CIVIL SERVICE.

LONDON:

HATCHARD & CO. 187 PICCADILLY,

Booksellers to H.R.H. the Princess of Wales.

1867.

LONDON:

STRANGEWAYS AND WALDEN, PRINTERS,

Castle St. Leicester Sq.

PREFACE.

This little Tale, which the Author has given permission to be published, was written more than five-and-twenty years ago, after a residence of six years in Marocco. The story is founded on tragical facts, which occurred at the time, and is intended to illustrate the character of the people of West Barbary, as well as the state of oppression under which the Jews of that country suffered, but which of late years the Author understands has been greatly ameliorated, owing to the humane exertions of Sir Moses Montefiore, and the remonstrances of the British Government.

April, 1867.

CONTENTS.

EXPLANATIONS OF ARABIC TERMS USED.

Alfa . . .	regiment.
Azora . . .	from Johor—Pearl.
Bab	gate.
Bintekee . . .	a gold coin (of seven or eight shillings).
Delal . . .	auctioneer.
Djehennem .	hell.
Djilabea . . .	a striped hooded cloak.
Douar . . .	a circle of tents.
Filelly . . .	from Tafilelt.
Fondak . . .	barrack—caravanserai.
Hayk	Moorish plaid.
Jinnah .	heaven.
Kaïd	a governor.
Kaisaria . . .	bazaar.
Kasba . . .	citadel.
M'Shouar .	audience hall—durbar.
Majnoon . . .	possessed with a demon.
Marabt . . .	holy beggar—friar.
Merjana . . .	coral.
Mulai Idris . .	patron saint of Fez.
Oom el hassn .	nightingale.
Peçeta . .	a silver Spanish coin.

Roh . . . . a spirit—(rook or castle.)

Rebeb . . . a stringed instrument.

Sahel . . . the plain.

Shah mat . . king is dead—(check-mate.)

Taleb . . . . a lawyer—scribe.

Zurzur . . . blackbird.

THE ARAB'S PLEDGE.

CHAPTER I.

THE CONSPIRACY.

OUR scene is in Marocco, and the reader will, I trust, pardon details of dress and scenery which may appear tedious, but are necessary in the delineation of the manners and customs of a people who, though so close at our doors, are so little known as the Moors, Jews, and Arabs of West Barbary.

The town of Marocco lies at the foot of the Atlas, which rises in grand, imposing masses to the eastward, piercing the sky with its snowy peaks. Around the town are extensive groves of date-palms, plantations of olives, gardens and orchards abounding with apricots, pomegranates, grapes, oranges, quinces, and jujubes, as well as flowers; which latter, however, are never cultivated with any care and grow almost wild. Beyond, extend the plains, varied by evergreen woods and tracts of cultivation, nearly to the sea-coast. These plains are barren during the greater part of the year, but after the periodical rains of spring, are

B

carpeted with grass and wild flowers; and afford
pasture to herds of gazelles, which at that season
forsake the vicinity of the rivers and bound joyously
over their free expanse.

The Jews, whom this tale principally concerns,
live among the fanatic Moors in a state of most abject
degradation. They are compelled to wear a distinguishing dress with the indispensable badge of a black
cap and shoes; they must take off their shoes and
walk barefoot in passing before mosques, official
residences, gates of towns, and in presence of any
persons in authority; the wealthiest Jews may be
loaded with abuse, and even struck by the lowest
Moors without daring to retaliate or raise their hand
in self-defence, the penalty for striking a Moslem
being amputation of the hand. On the slightest
pretext they are thrown into prison for the sake of
their wealth, and then tortured to extort a heavy
ransom for their deliverance. But their greatest
danger arises from the terms of the Mohammedan
law; in accordance with which if two witnesses swear
that a Jew has repeated the words of their confession
of faith, "I believe there is but one God, and
Mohammed is the prophet of God," his denial is worth-
less, as the evidence of Jews is not admitted against
Moors: he is at once invested with a Moorish dress
and forced to conform to Moslem rites, under peril, in
case of refusal or recantation, of being burnt alive.

The gardens before mentioned are the resort of the
towns-people, who come out to enjoy the coolness of

evening after the heat and dust of the streets. In one
of these a natural arbour was formed by several grape-
vines, which after climbing up the shafts of the date-
trees for fifteen or twenty feet had lost their hold, and
with interlaced boughs and tendrils, sloped back in a
curtain of foliage supported by thick shrubs of jujube
and arbutus, gemmed with waxen berries of yellow and
crimson; from the festoons above hung a profusion of
half-ripe, blushing grapes. The grassy floor of this
bower lay in deep cool shade. Two Moors had
selected this inviting spot to spread their carpet. In
front of them, where the trees had been cleared away
to plant the ground with melons and Indian corn,
opened an extensive view of the snow-capped Atlas
and the city of Marocco; its mud walls hidden by a
canopy of white dust and vapour, above which rose
the minarets of the mosques, the chief of which, the
Juma Kitibea, towered in proud pre-eminence.

These two persons, who are likely to be prominent
actors on our scene, showed by their dress and
appearance that they were soldiers of. the Sultan's
army. Over a coat of red cloth they wore a full white
shirt with open sleeves, confined round the waist
by a red sash, full white trousers to the knee, and on
the head a tall red cap with a blue silk tassel; yellow
slippers completed their costume, and over all they wore
the white hooded burnoose. They carried silver-
chased ataghans in their belts; their swords and guns
were leaning against the trees; their horses, with
saddles of faded red, were picketed among the long grass.

The elder of the two, Abdslem Ibn Hadj, was a short thick-set mulatto, whose grisly black mustachios and beard gave a fierce expression to a countenance which was otherwise a picture of treachery and cunning. The other was a young man of pale complexion, with a fine cast of features and a noble form; he was originally of an amiable and retiring disposition; but this had been greatly changed by his association with a dissolute soldiery. He was the son of a man of rank; his father had for many years been Kaïd of a large province, and being suspected of having amassed wealth, was, according to the arbitrary custom of the country, thrown into prison, his property confiscated, and his son forced to serve in the capacity of a common soldier. The father did not long survive his disgrace.

This oppression rankled in the heart of Hassan, and nearly overcame every remnant of moral principle in his mind. He saw that honour and religion were only used as a veil for the greatest enormities, and that self was the great idol of prince and beggar; watching every opportunity for revenge, he had become mixed up with Abdslem, whom he had foolishly trusted, in plots against the Sultan who had injured him.

The two friends, having filled their pipes with hashish, threw themselves on the carpet, while a negro boy, who had accompanied them on a mule, produced from his panniers provisions, dried fruits, and some charcoal, with which he made a fire in a hole in the ground to prepare tea,* an indispensable beverage in every Moorish party.

Abdslem, whose intellects were getting confused with the intoxicating drug he was smoking, began talking,—

"God is great! yes, God is great! oh, wonderful! What blessings He has bestowed on His servants! The infidels covet our country; of course, they have heard how beautiful it is; they can't help it. O the green grass and running water! Ya Mohammed! O the noble horses and the graceful girls! Curse on the infidels! Abdslem Ibn Hadj wears a sword! The banner of the Prophet waves over us! And where are their fathers' houses?"

He lay back emitting a thick cloud from his lips, without observing his companion, who was all the time immersed in a dark reverie, with his eyes fixed on the carpet pattern.

"God be praised!" he continued. "What a splendid view! Look at that mosque! they say its height is not to be measured. And look at God's hills; the true believers in Paradise enjoy not greater—"

Here he stopped short, perceiving that he was talking for his own amusement.

"How now, Hassan! do you come out here to shut your eyes, or to enjoy God's blessings? Better have stayed in your fondak smothered with dust and fleas.

* The diversity of national beverages is curious. The Moors drink *green* tea; the Persians, *black* tea; the Turks *coffee*; as the French affect *wine*, and the English *beer*.

I'll lay my life your head is still running on that infidel's daughter, (may her days be shortened!); you have no more heart than a Christian. O child! if the men got wind of it, you would be the laugh of the whole Alfa!"

He checked himself as he saw the other's darkening brow, which showed him he was going too far with one who, although his equal in station, was his superior by birth.

"Well, don't be offended, you know I am your friend, although *I am* fond of talking. Try this tea; the live water of the infidels I prefer, but that is not easily got."

"May your father's house be desolate!" said Hassan surlily, putting aside the offered refreshment. "Have I not curses enough on my head, without that of your rattling, insulting tongue superadded; if you have no better entertainment to offer, hold that in the devil's name?".

"Ya Allah! may the devil be accursed! This is all I get for my good will. The wise has said, ' He who loses his temper may drink the sea.' I am silent!" and calling the boy to replenish the tea-pot, he continued drinking cup after cup till he had exhausted the supply, while his companion sat evolving wreaths of smoke and twisting long grass into cords.

"And now," said Abdslem, turning suddenly round, "shall I prove to you that I am your friend?"

Surprised by this sudden address Hassan looked

up with an expression of hope on his face; which, however, quickly changed to a glance of suspicion.

"Why, Abdslem, if words could do it, you can; but I have long learnt the value of friendship, which is bought and sold like market stuff, but ever fails in time of need,—unless interested."

"Very good," said Abdslem; "so it is; but hear me first, and then judge. You love the Jewess! The Jews were created for slaves to the Moslems! But you can't buy her; the infidels won't sell their children with all their love of money; and she won't turn Moslem; so you can't marry her, it is against the Koran. She is pretty; it is a wonder how God can give Jews such beautiful daughters!"

"May your father be burnt! Why do you torment me thus?" said Hassan, springing up.

"Wait and hear me," said Abdslem; "I have a plan in which I will the more readily assist as it is to save a soul from Djehennem. Now mark! try your luck once more, and if she repulse you, we will go and swear that she has pronounced the confession of faith of Islam. The fear of death will prevent her from retracting; and you will then possess the object of your wishes at the trifling expense of an oath. There, have I proved I am your friend? God is great!"

Hassan, whose countenance had brightened when expecting to hear a way of obtaining the object of his wishes, although accustomed to wickedness, when he thus suddenly heard the proposal, revolted at its enormity.

"Friend!" echoed he.   "Fiend, say rather! I
thought I had fallen low enough; but I see there are
deeper depths of villany; and *you*, my *friend*—"
he continued, with a bitter sneer, "would still plunge
me downward, until you land me in the lowest pit of
hell; and there you would leave me,—if you may."

Abdslem was rather staggered at the manner in
which his proposition had been received.

"Wonderful," said he; "I thought to have served
you, and these are my thanks!   Well, I will trouble you
no longer with my friendship, or my company.   Find
another butt for your spleen; I have borne with you
thus long for your father's sake.   Here, bring my
horse, you son of fourteen generations of black fathers,"
he called to the slave boy.

Hassan was touched.

"Stay!" said he, seizing his hand, as he rose to
depart, "forgive me,—my misfortunes gall me; I speak
at random; leave me not now when I so much need
your assistance."

"I do not bear enmity," said Abdslem; "I only
thought of gratifying your wishes, but if you will not
take what may be had for such small pains, let us
think no more of the infidel.   I would rather see all
the Jews in Marocco burnt in their quarter than see
you down-hearted."

"I have trusted you, O my brother," said Hassan,
"with this secret grief; but can we not devise some
other means?"   For he was unwilling to give up all
hope.

"I see none," said Abdslem. "Open violence would cost you your head; and fraud would bring you under the Sultan's hand, and he would not spare your father's son. What worse are the means that I propose than the end you aim at? And then the merit of bringing a Kafir to the true faith!"

"True! there is some reason in that," said Hassan, whose scruples were fast fading away before his passion, which blinded his better judgment; and what had at first revolted him by its criminal deformity, softened down by familiarity and was stripped of its repulsiveness.

"True, she will thank me hereafter for saving her from infidelity."

"God be praised!" said Abdslem; "and you will laugh over it some day, when your 'pearl' is called Merjana, wife of Hassan; as a praiseworthy stratagem."

They now mounted their horses which were unwillingly disturbed from their unusual feast on the leafy drapery that surrounded them; and leaving the boy to collect their canteen, they rode slowly towards the town; and before reaching it the artful suggestions of Abdslem had completed the victory over his companion's scruples; and the next morning was fixed upon for putting their plot in execution. As they entered the gate called Bab Er Rahamna, the eastern sun threw their shadows far up the street, a symbol of the darker shadow that their coming cast upon their victim.

CHAPTER II.

THE ACCUSERS.

THE Jews living in the towns of Marocco occupy a walled quarter, separated by gates from the rest of the town; physically they are a fine race, many of them are very wealthy, and some of the best families show high breeding, but the cringing and servile habits, to which they are inured from infancy by oppression, have impressed their demeanour and physiognomy with timidity and cunning, and effaced in a great measure the higher and nobler feelings from their minds. There are partial exceptions to this, as in the case of some of their priests and men engaged in European trade, who are brought less into contact with their masters, and feel themselves under more protection. The separate quarter, although affording security in ordinary times, seems to enhance the danger to its inhabitants in time of trouble or insurrection, for the moment that the Sultan's authority is relaxed or in danger, the mob and the soldiery break loose; urged on by fanaticism and cupidity, the cry is, "To the Jews' quarter!" and the place is sacked, as by a foreign enemy. It is wonderful that men who can afford it, will submit to live with their families in this constant state of oppression and terror; but such is the force of habit and the love of gain,—for I can hardly place in the category the love of country,—that very few, or none, do leave it. It is true that the law does not permit them to leave the country, but they might easily escape or evade it.

The women, seldom leaving their houses, are less exposed to the degrading influences which lower the character of the men; their countenance is more open, and their bearing more independent; as a rule, they are good-looking, and their manners and address are graceful and ladylike. Although the prevailing colour of the race is Andalusian, there are not wanting many possessing the clear and brilliant complexion of northern climates, and even blue eyes are not uncommon.

In the Jewish quarter in Marocco, in a small house, distinguished only from those which surrounded it, by its cleanliness of exterior and neatness within, lived a Jewish matron with her only daughter; their appearance and manners showed them to have belonged to a higher station, though now reduced to the necessity of gaining a living by needle-work. The mother was the widow of a priest, who had been esteemed for his unostentatious charity, and who had bequeathed to his daughter little of worldly goods, but instead, a well-grounded faith in the Scriptural promises and a strong love for her ancestral religion. The child's personal beauty as she grew up was looked on by her parents— as it foolishly is by most parents—as a great blessing.

How little did they foresee, while doating on her loveliness, that they were fostering serpents that would one day sting her to the soul, and prove her most fatal curse. She was now about eighteen, a vision of grace and beauty. Most descriptions of beauty have been failures, and I will not add another to them by attempting it, but to see Azora, after her morning occupation of reading the prophets, her perfect cheek resting on her perfect hand, her large dark eyes cast upward, her lovely parted lips partially revealing their translucent gems, while a glow of enthusiasm lighted up her beautiful features; the only epithet by which to describe her beauty is "heavenly." Her dress was an embroidered spencer of pink damask, over a shirt of striped muslin, whose ample sleeves nearly reached the ground, and a frock of dark green cloth edged with gold lace. A crimson Algerian scarf encircled her waist, and silver anklets and bracelets attracted admiration to the limbs they could not adorn. A light green silk handkerchief was bound round her forehead, the ends hanging loose behind, and confined her hair, which fell down her back in long broad plaits. Her mother's dress was of a similar description, but of different materials; and, instead of her hair, which their customs will not allow married women to show, she wore the flat brush of black ostrich feathers fastened on each side of the face, under the head-dress. She was engaged in arranging the cushions of the divan and their few articles of household equipment, preparatory to their morning meal, when Azora tripped joyously in with several garments she was in course of embroidering on her arm, and kissed her.

"My blessing on you, my rose of Paradise," said Rachel.

"May *you* be blessed, O my mother!" returned Azora; "and see how much work I have done. Is it not well done?" and her merry laugh rang out musical, as she nestled down by her mother.

"Yes," said her mother, "we shall soon have earned enough for a dowry worthy of your family, though your beauty is dowry for a queen!"

Suddenly the girl stood up in an attitude of terror; her eyes fixed, and her hand pressed to her forehead.

"What is it, my child?" cried Rachel, "you frighten me; are you ill?"

"O my mother," said she, mournfully, "I had forgotten; I know not what brought back to my mind horrible dreams, which last night visited me, and which troubled me as the whisperings of evil spirits."

"You read too much, my child, and spoil your sleep; but let not dreams trouble you, mere fanciful flights of the imagination while reason sleeps."

"Yet it is written," she replied, "'In dreams, in visions of the night, when deep sleep falleth upon man, the Lord showeth His will, and sendeth warnings to His servants.'"

"May the evil be averted!" said her mother; "but cheer up, my child, and let us put our trust

in Him, the Holy One, who holds all under His
hand."

It was some time before Azora could shake off the
indefinite dread of impending evil which oppressed
her; but she gradually recovered her usual cheerful-
ness, and, after their frugal repast, they sat down to
their work.

In the course of the forenoon, a knock at the door
was answered with some hesitation by Rachel, who
gave admittance to our two acquaintances of yesterday.
With a lordly air of patronage they sat down, and re-
clined on the cushions at the end of the room.

"Peace," said Abdslem; "peace to all true believers. Well, daughter, is my caftan finished? I
have waited for it long. To-morrow there is a review
and powder-burning. I *must* have it."

"I trust it will be finished this evening," said
Rachel; while Azora, feeling their eyes fixed upon
her, bent down over her work; "and I hope my lord
will be pleased with it."

"No doubt about that," said Abdslem: "and I
hope you will be as pleased with your pay!" he added
sarcastically, with a look at Hassan; "but I shall
want more braiding in front; and you have not silk
enough. Here, Rachel," said he, in a commanding
tone, "take this dollar, and go to that enemy of God,
Benjamin, and buy enough to complete it; and hear!
don't let him cheat you!"

It had been concerted between them to dismiss the
mother, that they might have a clear field to put their

plot in execution; and she was no sooner gone, than Abdslem, feigning business at a house in the vicinity, and telling his friend to await his return, also departed. Thus left alone with one, of whose feelings towards her she was well aware, Azora naturally felt uneasy; her occupation had brought her into contact occasionally with Moors of this description; but she had hitherto managed, by the firmness of her behaviour, to keep them at a respectful distance; but the importunate perseverance of Hassan had caused her much misery and apprehension. Hassan arose; the struggle in his bosom was fierce and short: he paused; but his better feelings succumbed to the fire of his passion.

"Azora," he said, "Azora, I have poured out at your feet the love that devours me; you have repulsed me with contempt. Can my undying love not move you? Have you no pity? Can you see my anguish without one word of hope? Oh, how I love you! Azora! Azora, have mercy!" and he clasped his hands in supplication.

"This is folly," said Azora, who had risen to her feet. "You are a Moslem; I, a Jewess; what love can there be between us? Go! and crush out the wicked thoughts with which you insult me; but talk not of love:" and a deep blush overspread her beautiful face.

"You will drive me mad," said Hassan, with concentrated feeling, and his frame trembling with emotion. "Beware! for I will no longer be fooled; I am come now for the last time. If I go hence this day without a ray of hope, by the holy Koran I swear you shall live to find that Hassan's spurned love can only be matched by his hatred and revenge!"

"And is it so?" said Azora, recovering from her alarm at his increasing violence, but deadly pale. "Then know that I am no more to be intimidated by your threats than deceived by your professions. I know that I am exposed to your violence, but the Sultan's protection is spread over the poorest of his subjects!"

"Think not," said Hassan, "that I intend to break the laws. No! but the law itself shall place you in my power. And now decide," added he, in a lower tone, through his clenched teeth, and seizing her wrist in his grasp; "for, by the sword of the Prophet, I swear you shall be mine, or perish at the stake!"

"God of Israel! help me!" exclaimed Azora, as the horrible design now burst upon her mind. Regaining her self-possession, she replied in a calm tone, "Then let me perish! There is a God above who will exact fearful vengeance for innocent blood!"

"On my head be it," said Hassan, with unchecked rage; and seeing Abdslem, who was now returning, he rushed out, shouting, "Bear witness, O Moslmeen, this woman has professed the faith of Islam."

"I have heard it! I have heard it!" said Abdslem. "To the Cadi!" and collecting a rabble as they proceeded, they all went off to the tribunal of the Cadi, to seal by false witness their iniquitous plot.

On their departure, Azora stood riveted to the

spot, scarcely able to believe in the reality of what had occurred ; but a sickening chill came over her, as she began to recollect some part of the dreams which had so unaccountably affected her. Presently her mother returned, and, seeing her daughter pale and speechless, her hand pressed to her head, the purchases dropped to the ground, and she clasped her child in her arms.

"My child ! my child ! what has happened ? Oh, speak !"

"The dream ! O my mother ! The dream ! We are lost—lost—and ruined !" and, leaning her bursting head on her mother's shoulder, through sobs and tears she told her, in broken sentences, the conspiracy of the Moors against her honour and her life.

"Shall the curse cleave to our race for ever ?" said Rachel. "But, no; they shall not take you from me ; " and she clasped the affrighted girl more closely to her bosom, as they heard the sound of voices, and the approach of a crowd in the street.

"They cannot — they dare not !"

By this time the return of Abdslem, with the Cadi's soldiers, to summon Azora to the presence of that functionary, put an end to her lamentations ; and forgetting her caution and the usual respect to be shown to a Moslem, she endeavoured to assuage her grief by uselessly aggravating their oppressors.

"Oh ! may a mother's curse light on you and yours ! May your children be fatherless, and your wife a widow. Had your eye (sleepless be it ever) no pity ? Could you not spare my innocent child ? Perjured slave !

c

reprobate scum of the children of Edom — may every curse that ever came out of the mouth of man be poured in one appalling mass on your devoted head! O Lord of Hosts! hear me!"

These curses were poured out, half in Hebrew half in Arabic, as she stood with one arm round her daughter, and the other raised to heaven! She looked an inspired prophetess expecting the thunderbolt to seal her denunciation.

"Listen!" exclaimed Abdslem to the appalled bystanders —" be witness to her curses, and to me,— a Moslem!—Woman, your curses be on your own head. What is written will happen! If the Prophet, (on whom peace,) has enlightened your daughter's mind with the truth of Islam, and she wishes to leave your worn-out religion, what is it to me? The praise be to God, what is written must be!"

"A lie! he knows it a lie," said Azora. "I was born a Jewess, and so I will die! and I go not except by force!"

"Then force it shall be;" and with the help of the soldiers, and in spite of her screams and resistance, they tore her from her mother, who, overcome with anguish, swooned in the arms of the women who had collected and looked on in terror. Abdslem then threw her hayk over Azora (for he would not take a woman through the streets unveiled) and led her off in triumph, the crowd that followed chanting as they went along—

"La illaw il Allaw—
Mohammed er rasoul Allaw!"

Azora had often heard this chanted at the Moorish funerals, and she now felt it as the knell of death.

The Cadi was sitting in the gate of the town, where he usually administered justice; these gates have side arched recesses where the guards are quartered and are very convenient for the transaction of such business. The Cadi was a fine-looking old man, his white turban was without a plait, and he was enveloped in a fine woollen hayk. The crowd had been beaten off by the guards, and Azora stood before the Cadi almost unconscious of what was passing around her. The oaths of Hassan and Abdslem were carefully written down with a reed pen, and sworn on the Koran, which was reverently held above the waist, and then restored to the case in which it was kept. "God be praised!" said the Cadi, "God be praised. For you, my daughter, my heart is joyful for your conversion. Ya Mohammed — glory to the Prophet, he has saved you from Djebennem, your name shall be changed;—and Hassan, he is a good youth, Hassan,—and ‘ good Moslem,—he shall take charge of you, and instruct you in the Koran,—a good sponsor."

Hassan's countenance was beaming with satisfaction, and he already congratulated himself on his success; he little knew the heroic spirit that dwelt in that fair form.

‘ But I forget," said the Cadi, "we must go through the forms of the law,—I grow old. Sidi Abd-el-Kader-Jilelly, protect me. Come, my daughter, and repeat the profession of faith, ‘ La illaw—’"

Azora had stood motionless while her accusers gave in their lying witness, and an appalling sense of the danger of her position crept over her, as she found herself, a helpless girl, in such ruthless hands; but at this point she summoned resolution to speak.

"What these perjured men lay on my head," she said solemnly, "is false—*utterly false,* and never will I be guilty of becoming an apostate from the faith of my fathers!"

"May evil be averted!" ejaculated the Cadi, pushing his spectacles upon his forehead; "this is another story, and alters the case." And here he cast a glance of scrutiny at the witnesses, whose involuntary confusion showed him at once that the charge was false; but he was a Moor, and a fanatic, and covetous withal, and with such adepts at bribery, it required very little by-play to make him see his profit in the transaction. "Daughter," said he, severely, "they have sworn; they are Moslem—you cannot retract when you have once said it. Hear the law,"—and he again took the Koran from its case, and turning over the leaves, intoned a long passage in Arabic, "'If any shall confess the faith of Islam, and afterwards relapse, the infidel shall be burnt,' &c., &c. That is the penalty of obstinacy. Are you prepared to forfeit your life? Speak! I await your decision." But Azora remained stunned. "Away with the Infidel!" cried the Cadi. "To prison with her!" and the guards advanced to obey his orders. Just then a ray of hope flashed on her mind.

"Stop! my lord judge," said she; "I *will* not

submit to *your* unjust decision. I hereby appeal to our Lord the Sultan; *he* will see justice done to the helpless and oppressed."

This was her last resource. An appeal to the Sultan, publicly made, cannot be passed over, and she thus removed herself and her cause from the hands of her persecutors. Hassan was foiled, but, unwilling to expose his feelings in public, he hastily left the place, in no very enviable state of mind, followed by Abdslem. The Cadi, though feeling his dignity offended, was obliged to put a good face on the matter. Muttering some unscriptural phrases against the protection given by the Sultan to the infidels, he directed Azora to be consigned to the women of his own hareem until her cause could be submitted to the Sultan.

CHAPTER III.

THE PLEDGE.

S soon as Rachel recovered her consciousness, the poor mother looked round in vain for her child, and felt almost crushed by her desolation, but soon, with that elasticity of feeling so providentially given to her race, she began to turn over in her mind the means of rescuing Azora from what she could not conceal from herself was most imminent danger. She pondered long and deeply. The first object was to raise money; for, in a country like this, she knew that bribery was the first, if not, the first and last, means of success; and she at once began collecting all their little articles of jewellery, and what money was in her possession. ' While turning out the contents of one or two small trunks, in which she kept what she possessed of value, her eye was arrested by the sight of a small green velvet pouch, four or five inches square, ornamented with tarnished embroidery, such as is commonly used for carrying flint and steel.

"The Pledge!" exclaimed Rachel, her face brightening with hope; "as my soul liveth, this is not sent to me for nought in my hour of peril. The Arab's Pledge! Oh! he will save us! But where to find him?

Alas! he may be a month's journey in the Desert — but no! now I remember I heard that he was marching with the tribes against the south, and was already at Ta Filelt."

She immediately sent to call her daughter's betrothed, who was already on his way to the house, the intelligence of this outrage having quickly spread. These betrothals take place at an early age, and as young people, among the Jews, see a great deal of each other, their marriages, as a rule, are cemented by great affection, and attended with much happiness. Yusuf was a young man engaged in trade, who had been in the habit of travelling with small ventures in the provinces; he was strongly built, and accustomed to fatigue, and possessed considerable talent, with a large amount of caution and common sense. He was almost in a state of frenzy, which was aggravated by his knowledge of its impotence, as he listened to Rachel's description of the occurrence.

"O mother! dear mother! this is horrible, to be deprived at a blow of all that is dear to me. And oh! what must her sufferings be? Why are we such slaves?—but I will fly to save her! What is my life worth?" And the spirit of the man made a feeble attempt to rise within him. "The Sultan shall hear me, though he slay me!"

"Yusuf, my poor boy," said Rachel, "you can do nothing: are we not Jews? Your life would be thrown away, and in vain. What can be done with money, that I will do; listen to my voice, and if it please the

God of Abraham to help us, you may yet be the means
of her rescue."

" O mother! but tell me how ! "

" Listen—it is now seven years since that an
Arab prisoner fell into the Sultan's power. Through
my husband's assistance (God rest him!), he was en-
abled to make his escape; my husband also redeemed
his favourite black horse, which had been given to a
common soldier, and without which he refused to
escape. It was in the cool morning, before the sun
had risen, when my husband guided the Sheik out of
the town gates, where he found his steed ready saddled
for flight. The Arab, free, and once more possessing
his favourite, was moved nearly to tears. My husband
told me that the horse recognised his master, and that
their meeting was like the meeting of two sons of
Adam. The Arab then took my husband by the hand,
and thus addressed him : ' O friend, you have known
me as a helpless prisoner ; my faith was not your faith,
yet have you conferred on me benefits which I should
have looked for in vain from these Moors, who call
themselves Moslem. ·O friend! know me now as
Hamed Ibn Ishem, Chief of the *Woled Abou Sebah*.
Gold cannot repay the obliagtions conferred on my
father's son, but gold you shall have. But you are a
Jew, and here, are ever subject to danger and persecution, and evil days may come, (which God avert !) when
my assistance may be of service to you. Therefore,
you shall take a Pledge of me, that all the tribes may
know that we are brothers, and that the peace of God

is between us.' He then took this pouch, embroidered with his name, from his belt, and put in it a lock of hair cut from his horse's mane. ' Wherever you show this, every Arab will obey you. If you are oppressed, fly with your family to the shadow of my tent :— if in danger, send to me for assistance ; and as my faith has not prevented you from aiding me in my distress, I swear, by the God of Ishmael, that nothing shall prevent my redeeming this pledge at the risk of my life ! Peace be with you !' and, pressing my husband's hand, he sprang into the saddle, and was soon lost to sight in the morning mist. The Sheik sent us gold, but my husband's beneficent spirit would not allow him to enrich himself while there were poor to be relieved, and this pledge was almost forgotten, until to-day it came on my sight like a messenger from heaven. The hour of peril *is* come. Take it, my son—seek out the Sheik—he will redeem his pledge; many of our people live in their tents, and peradventure I and my child may escape to the wilderness, even as wandering birds cast out of the nest. Oh, let not to-morrow's sun see thee within ten hours' journey of this accursed city."

Yusuf had listened to this narrative with the deepest interest, but his mind did not jump so readily at the conclusion of the sanguine Rachel.

" This is sudden," he said, " and should I find the Sheik, he may deny his pledge after so long a time."

"Impossible !" interrupted Rachel; "an Arab will not refuse aid to an ordinary claimant, who seeks hos-

pitality in his tent. How can a Chief deny his pledge ?
If it were possible, he would be shamed and outcast
from his tribe ! But he will not ! ''

"I hope your confidence is well founded, but if
anything happened to Azora before my return ? O
mother, I must see her first.''

"No, my son," said Rachel, solemnly, " no !—not
as you value her life. But delay not, every hour —
nay, every minute is precious.''

"Well, mother, I obey you; but *you* must see
Azora, and tell her of my ceaseless devotion ; and oh,
entreat her not io be rash, but to gain time as long as
possible. Pray for me on this perilous journey, and
bless me, O my mother.''

"God bless thee, my son, even the God of Israel
bless .hee, and prosper thee in the way, and bring thee
back again in safety.''

They embraced each other affectionately ; and Yusuf,
putting away the pouch safely in his bosom, returned
to his own house, with a sad heart, to make a few
necessary preparations for his sudden journey. These
completed, he left word that he should be absent for
some days on a trading expedition, and, mounting his
mule, in less than an hour was wending his way
through the suburbs of the town, absorbed in grief,
but urged on by dread lest the fate of his betrothed
should be decided before his return.

It was the day appointed for a grand hunt, and
the Sultan was passing the time in an octagonal
pavilion in the garden of the palace, until everything

was ready to set out. Mulai Abd Errahman was about
forty years of age, of a swarthy complexion, with regular features, and a handsome black beard and moustache; his eye was of that mild expression which can
blaze out with terrific energy when excited by passion;
his forehead was broad, and surmounted by a turban
of fine muslin. The rest of his dress was not dis-
tinguishable from that of other Moors of rank, and
over all he wore the fine Filelly hayk, which fell in
graceful drapery to his feet.

He was now reclining on a Persian carpet, one arm
leaning on a pile of cushions, fringed and tasselled,
while the other hand held a small china tea-cup and
saucer; drinking green tea being the one occupation
with which the Moors fill up all their spare time, no
milk is used with this tea, but the loaf-sugar is always
put into the tea-pot. On the carpet was a polished
brass tea-tray, with an English service of green and
gold, and some plates of preserves.

The dome of the pavilion, supported on pointed
arches, was brilliantly painted in every variety of
arabesque, and the arches and cornices worked with
stuccoed mouldings, the floor was of lozenge-shaped
glazed tiles of various colours, and these lined the walls
to the height of several feet from the ground. The
doorway was shaded with grape-vines and jessamine on
trellises.

One of the Sultan's attendants now entered, and
with a deep obeisance announced that the Cadi El Faki
Al Maimon had something of importance to communi-

cate, if he might be allowed admission; and the Sultan, although vexed at the unseasonable intrusion, gave his permission, with the usual "Bismillah," and the Cadi appeared. He was motioned to a seat at the lower end of the carpet; he then proceeded to lay the case of the Jewess before the Sultan, with sundry invocations of God's favour on the Khalifa of the Prophet and protector of the faith; and added that the infidel had denied the facts, and appealed to his exalted footstool; and that such being the case, she was now removed from his jurisdiction.

The Sultan was not naturally blood-thirsty, but could be cruel when governed by revenge or cupidity; and after hearing the Cadi's statement it occurred to him, that it would save him trouble if he allowed the Jewess, whom he plainly saw had been falsely accused, to return to her own persuasion if it could be done without contravening the law.

"God is great! You say the woman denies the charge; (enlighten thy servant, O Mohammed!) Is it not written of the infidel, that he shall voluntarily repeat his confession before the Cadi and the Ameens to make the ceremony legal?"

"Wonderful! Our lord the prince can teach the law to us his slaves; but is it right to allow indulgence to the infidels, to the injury of the faith?"

"I will take care of the interests of religion, the cause is now before me, you are no longer responsible. Where is the infidel?"

"She must be arrived by this time," said the Cadi; "but if I might presume to advise—"

"Enough, priest," said the Sultan, with a movement of impatience, and a look that Al Maimon did not think it safe to brave. "You are dismissed from attendance."

"May blessings be increased on our Lord the Sultan," he answered, and left the presence, as Azora was introduced between two soldiers.

When a Jew, of whatever rank, is introduced to the Sultan, though it be to bring him presents, he is always brought in by two guards grasping his collar, and thrown down on his face, then dragged up again and held, as though he were a criminal. But guided by a natural feeling of respect for a woman, Azora was merely left standing on the carpet, and the attendants retired. She could not forbear trembling before one whose word was fate, and on an occasion of less importance would hardly have been able to bear up against her emotions; but she felt she was a champion of her faith, and collected all her courage for the emergency. The Sultan had taken up a letter, which he was listlessly reading, and by a sign gave her permission to speak.

"May the king live for ever!" she said. "I have been falsely accused by perjured men of forsaking the faith of my fathers. I have appealed to your exalted tribunal, and I now ask for justice in the name of God!"

At the first sweet sounds of that soft voice, the

Sultan had raised his eyes, and remained gazing at the beautiful vision that stood before him. The flowing veil which had concealed her person had allen, hanging in loose folds from her left shoulder; and as she proceeded, her large dark eyes were fixed on the arbiter of her cause, her finely modelled hand and arm were raised in invocation of the Deity, and then dropped slowly to her side. It was enough, her fate was irrevocably sealed. And a slight hint from his own evil nature had gone further in proving the soundness of the Cadi's advice, than if he had supported it by all the texts in the Koran. Invested with the most arbitrary power, and unaccustomed to any opposition in such cases, he stood on little ceremony, when his only feeling was, that he was conferring a favour. Rising, he approached her, with an air of gracious familiarity.

"Think you," said he, taking her hand, ' tha I can be such a traitor to our Prophet's cause as to allow such beauty to shine on infidels. Still I have the power to send you back free—and make your accusers' heads roll at your feet. It depends on you," he continued, drawing her towards him. "Give the command, which shall seal the death of your enemies —your own triumph—and my happiness!"

. "Mock me not, my lord," said Azora, extricating herself from his hold, as she perceived his meaning. "I am unworthy of my lord's notice. I ask not the death of mine enemies. I ask not my life at the price of degraded innocence. I ask but justice! And oh! for the sake of that just God, whom you profess to

adore, and who will bless the protector of the oppressed, oh, restore me to my poor mother! Save
me! oh, save me!" and she buried her face in her
veil, and burst into tears.

The Sultan's first impression was astonishment at
meeting with such a rebuff, and then his dignity was
offended by the boldness of her speech, but his anger
was checked by her grief, which even he could not
behold unmoved; he attributed it, however, to a
womanish fear of death; but was quite incredulous as
to her resolution holding out so far as to brave it. He
thought it better to give her time for reflection, and
throwing himself on the cushions, said mildly, "Your
fate is in your own hands. Think on your danger,
for *I alone* can save you." And summoning his attendants, he directed them to conduct her to the
hareem in the palace. Azora, her eyes streaming with
tears, hopelessly followed her guide to the women's
apartments, where we must leave her to gather strength
for the new trials which she foresaw awaited her.

CHAPTER IV.

THE HUNT.

THE description of a Moorish hunting party, though not altogether relevant to my tale, may interest my sporting readers, and will contribute to the picture of Maroqueen customs, which this book, in subordination to the tale, is intended to illustrate.

" Is all ready ? " said the Sultan, to his master of the horse.

" May my lord's saddle be exalted," said Kaled Ibn Othman, " all is ready, and your steed is waiting proudly for the honour of carrying the sacred person of the Prophet's Khalifa. May my lord's sport be prosperous ! "

" Ameen," echoed the attendants.

Having put on a pair of orange-leather boots, and received his burnoose and sword from his chamberlain, the Sultan mounted his horse, a milk-white barb, richly caparisoned with crimson silk and damask, embroidered in gold ; the broad stirrups, bit, and dagger-like spurs, plated with gold ; the tasselled collar round the neck, containing charms against the evil eye. Two other horses were led by grooms, one a superb mottled grey, with green silk housings ; the other a noble black, with white silk housings. The " shade-bearer " carried a large crimson velvet parasol, the badge of sovereignty, mounted on a twelve-foot staff, over the Sultan's head, and his guns, inlaid with gold, silver, and ivory, were carried by attendants on foot. All the troops that could be got together were drawn up in irregular lines, on each side of the road, with yellow, red, and green standards flying; and as the Sultan rode out of the gate, a deafening shout of "Allaw berk Ommr Seedee!" (Long life to our lord!) ran along the line until lost in the distance. After leaving the town, there was little regularity attended to in the march. A body of chosen horsemen went first in every picturesque variety of colour and costume according to the taste or means of the individual; some had red trappings, some green; there were swords, and silver-mounted guns, and ataghans, of different lengths and shapes, caftans of red, blue, and green, yellow boots or slippers, then stirrups, bits, and spurs, some gilt, some plated, and some polished steel; and burnooses white or blue. The only mark of uniformity being the pointed red fez, with blue tassel. The chief falconer followed on horseback, with his men on foot carrying cadges on which perched several pairs of Barbary falcons hooded; one favourite he carried on his wrist. After these came huntsmen, leading a number of large fawn-coloured greyhounds with black muzzles, followed by a motley crowd of Moors on foot, armed with guns and sticks, and a pack of dogs, mongrel and hound, for beating up the country.

Once on the plain, the usual mad riding began;

parties of ten, fifteen, or twenty horsemen charging at
full speed, and on reaching the Sultan, firing their
guns at his feet, and wheeling off to the right and left,
while others came up in successive charges.   This com-
plimentary custom is never omitted.   The Moors are
enthusiastically fond of this "powder play," as they
call it, the Sultan himself often joining in it.   On
such occasions he takes the centre of the line, and is
always allowed to be a neck ahead of the rest.   They
were obliged to desist from this amusement before
reaching the hunting ground; and after passing through
tracts of olive-plantations, they came to a plain studded
with clumps of trees, brushwood, and a few date-palms
stretching away to the foot of the mountains, and
where the battue commenced; the men forming a
long line beating the jungle.   The red partridge rose
in coveys at every point, and were knocked down by the
sticks of the beaters with great dexterity.   As the hares
broke, the hounds were slipped, and were scouring the
plain in all directions; there was no such thing as
regularity or fair play, for whenever the hares came
near the beaters they were shot, or disabled by a well-
aimed stick.   In another direction, in which the Sultan
rode, the falconers had come upon packs of sand-
grouse, a handsome game bird, as large as the red
grouse, with a very powerful flight.   The Barbary
falcon is a splendid bird, a little smaller than the Pere-
grine, but of great power and speed.   They are not
trained to "wait on," but as they were cast off, they
took the air, and darted like lightning into the

affrighted flock, each time bringing a victim fluttering to the earth. Altogether it was an animated scene, dogs yelping, huntsmen hallooing, falconers whooping, and horsemen galloping over the plain.

A country Berebber having reported a herd of antelopes feeding three miles off, a halt was ordered under a clump of trees, to consult on the best mode of approaching them, and for a short rest. Presently an altercation among the dismounted horsemen and others on foot attracted the Sultan's attention, the cause of which we will relate. They had fallen in with a wandering Marabt, in a striped cowled frock, studiously patched, to give it the appearance of raggedness and poverty; he carried a water pitcher over his shoulder by a stick, a welcome sight to the huntsmen, who had been exposed for the greater part of the day to a burning sun.

"God be praised," said Bozaffer, "who has sent us water so opportunely. — Peace," said he to the Marabt, "and excuse my begging your blessing, till I have blessed myself with a drink from your pitcher." And seizing it without ceremony, he took a long draught, then wiping his mouth, and taking breath, he continued, "When a man thirsts he is not particular, but I think the last well you drew from was well stored with frogs, for I swear a croaker kicked me on the nose when drinking."

The Marabt's sallow countenance became pale as he seized his jar, which seemed likely to make the round of the mouths present. "The blessing of Si Hamet o Moosa be with you, my children! Have I not a hot journey before me, and shall I not want water to sustain me? The land is dry and parched!" and he prepared to depart.

"Not so fast," said Abd el Aziz, catching the handle of the water vessel; "you are a Moslim, and cannot refuse water to Moslmeen who thirst; besides, is not the river within an hour's walk?"

The Marabt, however, seemed to have other reasons for refusing their request; but what could sanctity avail against a dozen men parched with thirst? They crowded round him, struggling to obtain possession of the jar, of which he would not loose his hold, and in the scuffle the fragile vessel was broken to pieces, and the coveted water was spilt on the arid soil. Bozaffer, who, having quenched his own thirst, had looked on encouraging his companions, now sprang forward, crying, "The frog! the frog!" and picked up a piece of reed, stopped at each end with beeswax, from among the fragments.

"Wonderful!" he exclaimed, as he opened one end, and drew forth a written scroll, which had thus been preserved uninjured in the water.

"Mashallah!" said the Marabt, in as calm a tone as his agitation would permit. "It is a charm to preserve me from the evil eye and the dangers of the road;" and he eagerly extended his hand to take the paper; but Abd el Aziz, who had marked his look of terror at the discovery of the scroll, and was enraged at seeing the water all lost, interposed.

"No, no! A curse on his father! He had good

reason for refusing water to the Moslim; he is no Marabt,—he is a spy!"

Here the approach of Kaled put an end to the dispute. Abd el Aziz gave him the paper, with an explanation, of the circumstances, and he, returning, communicated the same to the Sultan, to whom he presented the paper, holding it with the skirt of his burnoose. The Sultan, too much occupied with his sport to examine it at the time, thrust it into his sash, and ordered the Marabt under a guard to the tents. And the whole party of horsemen rode off in the direction of the antelopes; leaving those on foot, and the rabble to await their return. On nearing the ground the horses were concealed, and the Sultan and some good marksmen were placed in ambush among some brushwood and young date-trees, at a spot they knew the gazelles must pass to reach the open plains. Kaled and the horsemen then galloped off, and after a long détour, surrounded them by a line of men posted through the wood, which skirted the small plain on the opposite side, these were ordered to rush out on the first shot, and turn the game towards the ambush. Kaled and two of his men were conducted by the guide for about half a mile, creeping through the bushes; they then turned into a deep ravine, many of which, formed by the rains, intersect the plains. Before leaving the trees they had sighted the herd, about thirty-five, quietly grazing at a distance of half a mile. The Berebber scanned the course of the ravine, and marked every shrub and tuft of grass on its borders,

and his quick eye mechanically took in the bearings of
some of the prominent trees among which they stood,
he then directed them to follow in silence. After
creeping cautiously through the ravine, sometimes
making their way through the brambles, sometimes
cutting their naked feet among rocks, or helping each
other over holes and chasms, the gully began to shallow;
presently the Berebber stopped, he then whispered
Kaled, "You see that bush of Nebek in front, with
three thistle-heads growing through it? No? Now
look along this gun."

"Yes, I see," whispered the other.

"Inshallah! that is within one hundred and fifty
yards of the herd, you must creep up the bank on your
hands and knees; they will see you instantly, fire at
once, and may you be prosperous."

On reaching the spot the Moors raised their guns
on to the plain, protected by the tufts of grass, before
showing their heads to take aim; as soon as they did so
they caught the eye of the old buck, who with head
erect gazed for a second, and then uttering a loud
grunt, the whole herd bounded across the plain; but
not before the men had fired, two of them missed, the
third was more successful. The old gazelle who brought
up the rear of the herd stopped short as if stunned,
then turned to charge the Berebber, who was running
up to despatch him; but his legs were failing, the blood
gushed from his mouth and nostrils, and he rolled over
on the ground. The horsemen now came galloping
out of the woods, but the herd had already taken the

direction of the ambush, and were now out of sight. The Sultan and his party were losing patience at the long delay, when the shots were heard, and now, breathless with excitement, and with guns protruding from stump and foliage, the echoes had scarcely passed away, when the herd came sweeping down the glade, with heads thrown back, and their black shining horns and white sides and throats glancing in the sun; a moment they halted, as apprehensive of danger, before nearing the ambush, but the distant shouts made them again dash forward, the dead silence only broken by their pattering feet. Onward they came, till the beautiful creature in front of the herd was within fifty yards of the Sultan's stand, when he fired, and the animal springing six or seven feet into the air, fell dead on his back. A volley from the rest of the party sent the alarmed herd flying with increased speed, leaving five more maimed and struggling on the plain. These had their throats cut, with the usual formula, "Bismallah!" Without this they are not lawful; even birds must go through the same process, and should they be already dead, and no blood will flow, they are thrown away as unfit for food.

After sufficient adulation had been bestowed on the Sultan's skill, they returned to where they had left the foot-men, and the whole party took the road to the rendezvous. The gazelles and hares were slung on mules, and the partridges and grouse carried by the men on foot. After passing the plain, they came to a precipitous descent down to the Valley of the Tensift;

the slopes were clothed with the dark evergreen foliage
of the Argan, studded with trees of Sifsaf, whose leaves
appear of glittering silver; with a palm here and
there shooting into the sky. The banks of the river
were brilliant with wild flowers, and clumps of rose-
laurel (Oleander) were reflected in its waters. At a
distance down the valley was seen the white-domed
sanctuary of Sidi Bou Shaib, and near it, on a mound
under a spreading fig-tree, were the white tents,
pitched in a grove. The cavalcade wound slowly
down the steep path, satiated with sport, but were
tempted to cast off their hawks in pursuit of the ducks
and widgeons that rose in flocks from the islets and
pools. The instinct of water-fowl is very remarkable.
Directly the duck sees the falcon swoop, he shuts his
wings, and drops like a stone into the water, followed
by the hawk, who is only driven from the pursuit by
the splashing water. One falcon showed great saga-
city—having been twice baffled by this ruse, he took
his station on a crag bordering the stream, until another flight came swiftly down. Motionless, he let
them pass, and then, dropping from his position, shot
along the ground in their track, and overtaking them,
darted upwards, turned on his back, struck his talons
into the breast of his victim, and bore it off in triumph.
Arrived at the camp, the Sultan retired to his tent,
and the whole party, as the evening advanced, spread·
their carpets under the shade of the trees. The
soldiers collected in groups, to drink and smoke and
enjoy themselves after the fatigues of the day. It is

true the Koran forbids wine and spirits, but there is not a Moor, from the Sultan downwards, who does not indulge in them whenever they can procure them. Mandolines and other instruments were produced, and Arabian Nights' tales were recited; Arab ballads were sung and listened to with excited interest by the several parties.

"Ya Mohammed!" said Muctar, a Moorish soldier, "that old darwish Achmed is always dinning us with his Merjana and the Forty Thieves, and Kalifa the fisherman, which we and our fathers have been hearing since the days of Haroun Er Raschid (on whom peace). Now let us have a song. Sing, O Cassim, son of the Arab, sing a song of the tent. Had you as many fleas in your tents as we have in the fondak? if so, you were wise to leave them."

Cassim was an Arab from the south, who had settled in the province for some years, and had entered the Sultan's service as a soldier, not without lingering regrets for the scenes of his early home. Removing the pipe from his mouth, he took up the instrument—

"I will sing, O Muktar, what you cannot understand; but you will—the noise."

He then struck the cords, and broke forth into a song, evidently improvised for the occasion—a talent which is not uncommon among this people.

THE ARAB'S SONG.

"Oh, for my long-lost desert sands,
    Where the ostrich alone doth dwell

And no tree stains its broad expanse,
Save the date-tree by the well,
The well,
Save the date-tree by the well.

Oh ! why did I leave the desert wide
In gloomy towns to dwell ?
And the black tents of my father's tribe,
And the maiden by the well,—
The well,
And the maiden by the well ?

There, is naught to break the desert fair,
As far as the eye can see,
And the Arab is lord of earth and air ;
Oh, the desert is for the free,—
The free,—
Oh, the desert is for the free !"

"Ya Beledee ! O my country!" said Cassim, as he
laid down the mandoline, "when shall I again see your
bright sands?"

"Adjaib, oh, wonderful," said Muktar; "if your
country was such a land as this, with wine and oil,
fruits and flowers, and running water, you might love
it; but a barren desert!"

"The desert is for the free!" re-echoed Cassim,
with a contemptuous smile. "What is your country,
with all its beauties? The home of slaves! The peasant sows, but who reaps? yet even he loves his country. The Arab's fare of milk and meal, and dates,
with liberty, is it not better than feasting without?
His goats' hair tent is healthy and clean, protects him

from all weathers, and contains those who are dear to
him. Accustomed to gallop in freedom over trackless
wastes, even the air he breathes in other lands oppresses
him, and is too close and confined for his expansive
feelings. The desert for the Arab, the town for the
drudge. God is great!"

"Hear him, O Moslim," said Muktar; "he speaks
like a priest, but give me the rebeb; here goes, for a
soldier's song:—

MOORISH SONG.

" Charging steeds, and beautiful girls,
    And the wine in the glass that laughs ;
Are joys unbought by gold or pearls,
    So I sing to my friend who quaffs.
       Refrain—Qua ha ha: ha ha ha: ha haffs,
         La ha ha: ha ha ha: ha haffs.

The wine laughs out with a ruby eye,
    The sweet girl, with a soft eye black ;
From my courser's eye the bright sparks fly,
    As he speeds like the cloudy rack.
          Qua ha ha: ha ha ha: ha haffs,
          La ha ha: ha ha ha: ha haffs.

After madding race, I reach the place
    Where my houri, in crystal slim,
Gives me rosy wine, with smiling face,
    When her lips have first kissed the brim.
          Qua ha ha: ha ha ha: ha haffs,
          La ha ha: ha ha ha: ha haffs.

Then joy to the horse, with the rushing feet,
  To the girl whose dark eye laughs ;
And joy let us drink, in the red, red wine,
  Thus I sing to my friend who quaffs.
            Qua ha ha : ha ha ha : ha haffs,
            La ha ha : ha ha ha : ha haffs."

"A song of Paradise!" said Cassim; "these are also God's blessings, O Muktar; some love one thing and some another."

Calls to horse now stopped their further amusement, and, striking their tents and collecting their carpets, they were soon all mounted, and accompanying the Sultan on his return to the town.

CHAPTER V.

THE SPY.

THE Sultan being sufficiently recovered from his fatigue, was reclining in his half-open tent, when it occurred to him to examine the paper which had been taken from the Marabt. He opened and began reading it carelessly, but before he had finished, his face was livid, for it proved that treachery was at work among his own personal attendants.

"God is great!" he ejaculated, "God is my protection. A conspiracy! The address — Abdslem Ibn Hadj,—the slave! And the seal, Sheik Hamed of the Lion Tribes!" then raising his voice, "Who waits?"

"My lord's slave," answered Abd el Aziz, who was on guard, and coming forward.

"The spy that was taken this morning, let him be taken outside the camp and return to me with his head!—Go!" said the Sultan.

"On my head and eyes;" and Abd el Aziz receiving a token from the Sultan, went out immediately to obey his orders.

The guards whom he summoned, astonished and awed by the sudden command, mechanically obeyed, and in spite of his prayers and entreaties the Marabt was forthwith decapitated, and his head, still dripping with blood, carried by the lock of hair on his crown,

and laid by Abd el Aziz in view of the Sultan, saying,
"Behold the traitor's head! thus perish the enemies of
the Khalifa!"

"God be praised," said the Sultan, counting his
beads. "It is well; so far. Approach and mark—
Take that head, mount your horse and ride to the
town; cause it to be nailed up over the gate of the
Kasba, and let it be proclaimed that he was a traitor
and a spy of your lord's enemies. That done, seize our
slave Abdslem of the guard, and lodge him in a dungeon, in chains, with hand torture. Here is my sig-
net, have I not trusted thee? and thy fidelity shall be
rewarded."

Abd el Aziz prostrated himself, kissed the seal
and placed it in his vest. "My lord's slave is too
highly honoured, in being the bearer of the least of
my lord's commands. May I ever deserve my lord's
favour!" He then left the tent, mounted his horse,
with the bloody head dangling at his saddle-bow, and
with heart elate, galloped to the town, entertaining
himself with visions of the promotion and honours he
was to derive from the Sultan's favour, of which, however, that head might have taught him the uncer-
tainty.

Rachel, although she had despatched her intended
son-in-law on his mission, left no means untried in the
interval to save her child. She first went round to all
the most influential persons of her own persuasion,
imploring their assistance and begging them to peti-
tion the Sultan for her daughter's liberty. The Jews,

on occasions of this kind when the integrity of their faith is menaced, always hold together for mutual protection, and are not sparing of money or exertion to prevent such precedents being established. The present outrage had caused a great sensation, and a large sum of money was at once collected with which to present themselves before the Sultan, and intercede for the liberation of Azora. Under any other circumstances, this would have succeeded, even had there been any truth in the accusation; but as the case now stood, it ultimately proved abortive.

The poor mother now repented the rashness of her language towards Abdslem; and the reason that worthy did not notice it was, that he foresaw she would be driven to the necessity of purchasing his friendship, or buying him off; he also meditated extorting money from the Jews for the same purpose, and his avarice had chiefly prompted him to make use of Hassan's passion to induce him to become Azora's accuser. Rachel, prepared to submit to any humiliation which would help to save her child, took her way in the afternoon through a retired part of the town to Abdslem's lodging. He was sitting in a small white-washed room on a smaller carpet, the only furniture was a mattress on the floor, and a copper ewer and basin; his gun, saddle, and sword, occupied a corner. Smoking his pipe of hashish he was ruminating on the golden harvest he should reap, from the traitorous connexion he had established with certain Sheiks of the Arab tribes, when Rachel entered.

" Welcome to the daughter of the infidel!" said he,
with an inquisitive look, as she gathered up her hayk
and sat down at the threshold. " She has repented of
her curses. She might have been punished, but Abdslem
is soft-hearted; what of Azora?"

" 'Tis that which has brought me to my lord's
presence," said Rachel. " When I uttered evil words
against my lord, I spoke with the mouth of fools, but
my lord is kind and has forgiven it."

" God is merciful; that is past, my heart has been
heavy for the evil that has befallen your daughter.
Why should I injure her? is she not a houri? That
renegade Hassan was the cause, that is—"

" My lord admits she was not guilty," said Rachel,
catching at the hint thus intentionally thrown out.

" God is great!—not exactly—but if I can help
her, I will do it for the love of God."

" What easier, my lord, than to proclaim her innocence?"

"And so lose my own head! Ah! the infidel's
gratitude. Shall I perjure myself and brave the Sultan?
Is not Azora in his hareem? If I were not so poor, I
have friends at court, whom I might pay for their
interest and intercession. But without money—Moors
are Jews—no better."

" You shall have gold," exclaimed Rachel, deceived by his apparent feeling. " I have some hundred
dollars; do for us what you can, and blessings attend
my lord. When and where shall I find you?"

" An hour after evening prayer, I shall be here,"

said he, scarcely able to conceal his satisfaction. "It shall be a sacred trust, and may it be the means of serving your cause."

Rachel's heart was too full for utterance, she kissed the hem of his dress, and rose to depart, when the door was thrown rudely open, and Abd el Aziz unceremoniously entered, without the usual "Peace be with you!" (It is the height of impropriety for a Moor to enter another's house uninvited.)

"So, you are Abdslem Ibn Hadj," said he.

"But whose dog's son are you," cried Abdslem, springing up and laying his hand on his gun, "that dare to break in on the sanctity of my dwelling?"

"You shall presently repent of your abuse, O son of a black slave! but now I advise you, to make your hand and gun more distant relations if you care for your head; which is likely soon to ornament the Bab el Kasba, by the side of a friend of yours. Do you know *that?*"

"The Sultan's seal!" exclaimed the astonished Jewess, while Abdslem started back terror-struck; his dark cheek blanched and his thick lip quivered as he saw the near punishment of the crimes of which his conscience accused him; and when Abd el Aziz, satisfied with the impression he had produced, ordered him to follow, he obeyed almost unconsciously. In the street he was seized by the soldiers who were in waiting and dragged to prison, and until he should be finally disposed of the following temporary punishment was inflicted on him. His hands were filled

E

with quicklime and salt, and then sewn up in raw hide, which, as it dries, binds the hand like a vice, while the caustic contents eat into the flesh and cause the most excruciating pain. He was then heavily ironed and thrown into a damp dark cell, where we will leave him to meditate on his misdeeds, while we accompany Yusuf to the Desert.

CHAPTER VI.

THE SAHARA.

ROM the inquiries he had made, Yusuf learnt that the Sheik of the Woled Abou Sebah was encamped on the borders of the Sahara, between the provinces of Suse and Draha. He had, consequently, taken a course through the mountains south of Marocco, where they begin to fall in lower ranges, towards the sea-coast. The inhabitants of this country are Berebbers, living in small villages, among whom he had been in the habit of travelling on trade; and as they were under the Sultan's government, there was little danger to be apprehended. After three days' travelling, almost day and night, he found himself on the south of the mountains. There were no more fixed villages. The few inhabitants of this wilderness, in which vegetation was rapidly disappearing as he advanced, were living in tents where wells of water were to be found. Resting at one of these stations, he had to make up his mind as to his onward course. The sum of his intelligence was, that the Sheik's camp was a day and a half journey in the Desert to the south-cast; and that a large caravan from the north was hourly expected on its way across the Desert to Timbuctoo. His object was to join this caravan, which he had hoped to have fallen in with before; and as they usually pay blackmail to the Arabs, when they are allowed to pass unharmed, he knew he should thus have no difficulty in obtaining their guidance to their Sheik.

From these poor peasants he could not obtain a guide, and he dared not offer them money, which he knew was a certain inducement for them to strip and perhaps kill him. His mule, too, was showing signs of fatigue, from the rapid and unaccustomed journey. At daylight, after taking the most minute directions from his host for striking the track of the caravan, he set off with a stout heart, his mule ambling from four to five miles an hour; and while the sun was yet far from noon, he found himself launched on that inland sea which stretches with little interruption from the Atlas to the Niger. With some of the instinct of the Arab, he guided himself by the aid of rising grounds, sand-hills, and indications left by bleached bones, sun-dried manure, and some rocks, keeping a straight course by the sun; but his heart sunk as the afternoon wore on, and no signs appeared of the desired tracks. Had the caravan not passed? or had it passed, and the wind swept the sand over its track and effaced it? He could travel on, but what probability of discovering the road, in such a waste? He might travel another day, and be able to return with safety, if unsuccessful; but then to lose the object of his journey, death were better.

He dismounted and sat down to think. The western sun threw the shadow of his mule far from him, and despair began to creep over his spirits. Hark! was that a shout? His heart bounded at a human voice in such a place, whether of friend or foe; it was welcome. He sprang up, and scanned the horizon. Another long, clear call, and at a distance of three-quarters of a mile he perceived some large fragments of rock, which he had not before noticed; on their highest point, and partly relieved against the sky, stood a dark figure, waving a cloth with one hand, with what seemed to be a gun in the other. If there had been danger, there was no escape; but Yusuf, accustomed to place confidence in these people, joyfully mounted his mule, and hastened to the spot.

The Desert Arabs, to whom I would now introduce the reader, are quite a different race from the Moors, and have little in common with the Arab population of the Maroqueen provinces. The latter have occupied these countries, on occasions of depopulation from plague, have adopted a settled life, and become partially identified in manners and dress with the people who surround them.. The Arabs of the Sahara retain their distinguishing characteristics.

Their dress is a blue tunic of India long cloth confined at the waist by a leather belt; besides swords and dirks, they carry double-barrelled guns, which come to them from the French settlements in Senegal. The complexions of the men are swarthy; their features are regular and strongly marked; they wear their hair in short curls, and the beard is usually short. They are decidedly a handsome race, and the beauty of the women is proverbial in the adjoining countries, "Dim el Arb" (Arab blood) being a common expression for female loveliness. They are brunettes, but their dark eyes and resplendent teeth are unrivalled. Their living is frugal — dates, barley-meal, milk, and cheese: flesh is used sparingly, though a sheep is always killed when a guest is to be entertained; the flesh of the gazelle and the ostrich, as well as that of the camel and sheep, is cut in strips, and dried in the sun for household supply.

When Yusuf came up, he found four Arabs sitting under the shadow of the rock, regaling themselves on dates and barley-cakes, spread on a piece of old garment on the sand, by the side of which was a small goat-skin of water. They were on an ostrich-hunt. Their guns were leaning against the rocks, and their horses picketed behind them. These horses were what an Englishman would call "bags of bones;" but they had magnificent points, were as hard as iron, and had eyes like lamps.

Yusuf immediately took his place in their circle with the salutation of "Peace!" This at once enlisted their good-will.

"Peace: behold the Jew: he hath put trust in us; he hath no fear."

"The children of the Sahel do not injure their guests; I have travelled since morning fasting; hunger will make the fawn brave."

"God's protection is over you," said another.

"Eat!—behold the food God provides is before you."

Yusuf looked round at them and at their slender store of provisions.

"You are four," he said; "your hunting may be prolonged; before the setting of to-morrow's sun you may be in more want of it than I. Direct me on my way; hunger can be borne."

"Art thou not an infidel?" said a third. "Hast thou no trust in God? Cannot God, who has sent us to your assistance, likewise provide us with food when we are in need of it? Eat. O Jew! eat. He who breaks not bread with the Arab is not the Arab's friend."

"Bismallah!" said Yusuf, at this conclusive argument, joining at once in their hard fare. He then asked, "Has the Soudan Cafila passed, or is it expected? and am I far from its track?"

"We have just left the track," said the Arab, who had last spoken; "the Cafila was to reach the last halting-place"—here he pointed north—"last night. They will rest at mid-day, and should soon be here. But, O Jew! have you goods in the Cafila? Behold, we have broken bread together; take your camels and return, for danger is before you. The Sheik of the Sebaïc is at war with the Sultan. Lo, you are warned; our faith is clean."

"Your bread is sacred; hear the truth; I have no goods nor camels; I go to seek the tents of the

Sheik himself, and only accompany the Cafila until I can procure a guide thither."

" If so, you have started in a fortunate hour. I will direct you; when you come to the second well in the desert,—should nothing happen before, for we know not what is written,— ask any Arab to guide you to the Chief, for he is not far thence. Be cautious, though you have nothing to lose — you travel with merchants. Remember the proverb, ' If you put your head in bran, the fowls will peck it.' Lo! I see the Cafila approaching."

Yusuf turned his eyes in the direction where the smooth desert was broken into low sand-hills, among which the long train was seen slowly winding onwards, and, although at a great distance, the loaded camels and their drivers could be seen, magnified by the evening mirage, like gaunt spectres against the horizon.

" May you be rewarded, friend," said Yusuf; " I am warned; but the infidel puts his trust in God."

The Arabs smiled as Yusuf remounted, and with salutations of Peace, he rode off; and before it was dark had joined the Cafila.

These caravans are composed of traders, who periodically assemble to traverse the Desert in company for mutual protection. They sometimes take guards, but their chief security is in the tribute they pay to the Arab tribes through which they pass. They carry manufactured goods and wares to Soudan and Timbuctoo, bringing back in exchange ivory, gold-dust,

ostrich feathers, gums, and slaves. They number from
five hundred to a thousand camels. These large
caravans are called *Akaba*. I use the word Cafila as a
more familiar term, and as applied to a smaller expedition. The persons composing the present one not
having yet experienced much of the hardship of
Desert travelling, were in great spirits. The camel-
drivers and muleteers were singing and chanting
verses of Arabic songs, improvised or from memory,
which were answered by others more or less wittily,
and drawing shouts of laughter from all within hearing. The singing encourages the camels to quicken
their pace, and contributes to the gaiety, by the measured time of their bells.

About twenty horsemen had escorted the Cafila
hitherto, but were to leave them a couple of stages
further, as it is only horses trained to it from colts
that can live on the Desert. Others were discussing
the rumours of war between the Sultan and the Chief
of the Arab tribes, which had excited in them the
greatest alarm.

" By the tomb of Mulai Idries," said a little rotund
fat Moor from Fez, with a florid complexion and long
white beard, which his fingers were continually comb-
ing; and mounted on a tall ambling mule. " By the
tomb of Idries (may his sanctity be increased !) if I
had heard this news before, I would have sacrificed all
the gain on these camel-loads before I would have left
my shop in the Caisaria, and then, perhaps, to lose our
life also, by the hands of these blood-thirsty Arabs;

who knows what is written, Allaw Kereem ? " and the little man's hands kept time with his increased agitation.

"In the name of the Prophet, uncle Mohammed," exclaimed a Marocco horseman, with a long gun across the pommel of his saddle, " you cry out before you are hurt. You are rich ; I am a beggar ; but are we not strong enough to send a whole tribe of these Arabs (the curse of Mohammed upon them !) to their fathers' graves, if they can find them in this sea, where you may lose sight of a camel for an hour, and not find him in a month ? " And laughing at his own bald wit, he turned to another horseman, who, from his northern accent and striped djelabea, the hood of which was drawn over his head, seemed to be from the neighbourhood of Tetuan ; he was mounted on a raw-boned horse, like those of the ostrich-hunters, and was at the time loading his gun.

"What say you, friend ? You seem prepared for work, but I trust there is no cause for fear."

The other looked up sharply at the speaker from under his hood, and went on with his occupation, saying,—

"He that despises his enemy is not wise ; he that reviles a people in their own country is not wise ; for sands as well as walls may have ears. I cannot talk, —when time serves, I may act. Danger there is, but as for cause of fear,"—and he once more looked at his companion's face, which had waxed paler—"it does not seem required in your case."

The horseman, whose name was Mohammed, galled by the reproof, but not daring to resent it, drove his spurs into his horse, which plunged forward and brought him in contact with the mule's load, a projecting part of which caught the folds of his dress, causing a large rent, and exposing a belt he wore next his person. This did not escape the other's quick eye, though he appeared to take no notice. The moon was a few days old, but the light of a clear, starry sky was sufficient on these white plains, and they travelled on until midnight, when they arrived at some wells, and halted. These wells were of a great depth, and the water was drawn from them in small leathern buckets, and poured into a stone trough, the exhausted camels biting, kicking, and pushing, in their eagerness to reach the coveted fluid. As the camels were watered, their fore knees were tied up, to prevent them straying, and they were turned loose to graze, on what few thorny plants they could find, while the men rolled themselves in their hayks, and were soon asleep, undisturbed by the roaring of camels, the shouts of the drivers, and the confusion which lasted for hours.

At daylight the march was resumed, but the party seemed to have lost their spirits; the song was hushed, and nothing was heard but the vociferations of the drivers, urging on their beasts, while the merchants plodded on silently, their heads enveloped in burnooses and large turbans, as a protection against the sun. About noon they came to a firmer soil, and the guides gave notice that they were approaching the halting-place, while the spirits of all were exhilarated by the prospect of reaching rest and water. Yusuf remembered the warning of the Arab, indicating these wells as the place of danger. About an hour's ride a-head, they could see masses of rock and brushwood on the plain, and when about a mile from this, the man on the spare horse rode forward to borrow a flint to put in his gun; and, whether by accident or design, it went off. A movement was now seen among the rocks, and spears and shining gun-barrels protruding above them, showed the place to be occupied.

"We are betrayed!" ran from mouth to mouth; "A signal!" "Down with the Kafir!" and they surrounded the horseman who had fired the shot. He remonstrated against their quarrelling amongst themselves, but was only met with cries of "Down with him!" "Drag him off his horse!" when, seeing they were determined on violence, he suddenly stripped off his striped cloak and turban, hurling them, with the gun he had fired, far away with his right hand, while his left held his bridle and a short double gun; his blue frock showed him to be an Arab.

"Back, slaves!" he shouted, in a voice of thunder; "I am Ali the Falcon!" and a smile of scorn was on his face, as the crowd recoiled before him, "let wisdom be with you. You thought *me* in *your* power—you are in mine—resistance is useless, offer none, and I pledge my word that you shall all return unharmed in person; the word of Ali el Bezz is sacred. Resist, or draw blood,—and may the curse cleave to my father's tents if every soul of this company shall not die this day!"

The crowd were panic-struck; some knew him, and all had heard of his daring deeds and wonderful escapes. The majority, who had not much to lose, were content to save their skins, but the rich merchants were loth to lose their all without a struggle, but were feebly seconded by the soldiers. At this critical moment, a band of thirty or forty horsemen, breaking the silence of the Desert with their united war-cry, " Allaw hu ackbaār !" their guns poised above their heads, rushed down at full speed, through a cloud of dust, on the affrighted travellers, while Ali, overlooked in the confusion, galloped out of the throng, and joined his band, who, seeing no appearance of resistance, had come to a halt.

"You should be more cautious," said Ali to his lieutenant; "not show your teeth before you can bite. You nearly sent me to heaven across the edge of a knife."

" It was not a fortunate hour, and you have escaped the houris ! To keep these fellows quiet when plunder is in view, were to keep fire in a goat-skin. But, by the Prophet, we may lose our prize yet."

The score of horsemen belonging to the Cafila had ranged themselves in front, thinking, by a show of resistance, to intimidate the Arabs, and make terms; but these, with Ali at their head, immediately dashed forward, standing erect in their stirrups, ready to pour in a volley, but the Moors, seeing their determination, at once turned their horses' heads and fled.

" Shame upon them !" said Ali; " they are soldiers

—they are Moslem—they abandon their trust without a blow. Yes! slaves are cowards! Will they not tremble when Sheik Hamed rides to the gates of Marocco? Now mark! my word is passed for their safety, on submission. I have other game afoot." And putting his horse to speed, he disappeared across the plain in the direction of the flying horsemen.

The Arabs, meeting with no resistance, dismounted, and proceeded to secure their plunder, stationing half-a-dozen pickets to prevent a surprise. The Moors and camel-drivers were stripped of everything that was of value, and the camels with merchandise were collected and made to kneel down by themselves. The Arab left in command galloped about superintending the disposal of the spoil, recommending submission and promising protection.

The old Fez Moor, finding that no one was killed, consoled himself in his fatalism, ejaculating as he was stripped,—

"It is written! God is great! It is written!"

Others, seeing the robbers were so forbearing, were less patient, but for these a hand on the dagger was an unanswerable argument.

Yusuf had been a patient spectator of the scenes which had been enacted, but it now came to his turn, and one of the robbers approached to strip him.

"Friend," said he, "offer me no violence. I am under the protection of your Sheik Sidi Hamed Ibn Ishem. My journey is to meet him. In his name, forbear."

"Infidel dog!" said the robber, "this trick shall not save your gold; you would give a drop of blood for every copper rather than part with it. You know the reward of resistance;" and he seized the defenceless Jew.

"Stop," said another, "we may repent, if the infidel speak truth. Jew," said he to Yusuf, "you come alone; have you no token?"

"I have," said he, "but it is as my life; take me to your leader."

They led the way to where the Arab was resting among the bales, with his bridle in his hand.

"I have claimed the sanctuary of the great Sheik," said Yusuf; "it has been refused me. A token has been demanded of me; lo, there it is."

He took the packet from his vest, and uncovering the velvet pouch, gave it to the Arab; the man, seeing the cypher of the Sheik, immediately kissed it, put it to his forehead, and returned it to Yusuf.

"It is enough," he said; "he is our brother; give him the best mule in the Cafila, and whatever he desires. Behold! he is under the shadow of the tent of Sidi Hamed."

The news ran from mouth to mouth, and there was nothing now they were not anxious to do to serve the Sheik's guest, and his newly-acquired influence was used to'intercede for some of the merchants, when he saw them too hardly used.

"Hast thou not bitten off thy tongue?" said the

robber to the other who had assaulted Yusuf, "better for thee, than to have reviled the Sheik's guest—the unbeliever has a big heart, make your peace."

"I am in the hands of God, Astofer Allaw," said the other.

CHAPTER VII.

THE SHEIK OF THE LION TRIBES.

LI, who was the Sheik of the douar that had plundered the Cafila; and had gone in pursuit of the flying soldiers; soon discovered Mohammed, all alone, and urging on his fatigued horse, which had no chance of escape from the enduring animal ridden by the Arab, whose object was, not to injure the soldier, but to secure the belt he wore round his person; so that, when within fifty yards of the chase, he called out to him to stop at his peril, promising quarter on submission.

Mohammed, recognising his travelling companion, and not daring to trust him after what he had said, checked his labouring horse, and, turning round in his saddle, levelled his long gun and fired, but with uncertain aim. The Arab muttered a deep curse as his horse fell under him, and, springing to his feet before the Moor could recover his speed, he had fired with a firm footing. Mohammed reeled in his saddle, his gun and reins dropped from his weakened grasp, he snatched at the pommel, and rolled over on the sand. The horse, missing his rider, stopped short, and stood foam-covered and panting with fatigue.

Ali, seeing his enemy fall, turned to his own horse, and a short examination showed that he would not rise again. The ball had struck his shoulder, and glanced inwards. The Arab sat down opposite his favourite, and buried his face in his hands; he thought of the many years he had stood at his tent, and the many perils from which he had saved him. He might have another, he might get a better, but it would not be the same. The wounded animal raised his head, in a weak effort to take a last look at his master, while large tears rolled from his bright eyes down his face.

"Poor Gazelle! O my child—you want but speech. God is great! It is written!—we must part!" and he retired a few paces to witness the end of his favourite. The expiring horse made a sudden plunge to regain his feet, but fell back powerless, his bright eye filmed, a convulsive struggle came over his frame, he groaned heavily, and died.

"You are avenged," said Ali, as he walked slowly to where Mohammed was lying; "for you, your doom was just. God is great!—his curse has fallen on his own head; his money has cost him his life,—and never will *his* children find their father's grave."

He unfastened the belt which the Moor wore under his clothes, and he found it was padded with doubloons and bintikee; he also stripped him of the principal part of his clothing; burnoose, caftan, and turban being of no use to one whose bones would bleach the desert till the judgment; and throwing the things across the Moor's jaded horse, he took a last look at his faithful

companion, and returned with a heavy heart to rejoin
his band, an additional pang going through him as the
dark shadows of the vultures, descending from the blue
vault, passed and repassed him, sharply defined by the
sunlight on the white plain. The camels had been all
reloaded, ready to start, escorted by the Arab horsemen.
The plundered merchants, with a few sorry animals
which were restored to them, and with sufficient provisions to serve them on their return, were left to retrace
their steps to Marocco. The night was now setting in,
and the band, accompanied by Yusuf, who was mounted
on the tall mule that had belonged to the little Fez
Moor, struck across the desert, travelling by the light
of the stars, with an occasional rest, till morning; and
as the sun rose, clear and warm, above the level of the
horizon, they came in sight of the head-quarters of the
Arab Chief, situated in a sort of depression of the
ground. This spot was called *Ain El Khmmis*, from
five wells, which afforded an invaluable supply of water.
Myriads of black goats'-hair tents covered the plain,
pitched in circles, or hollow squares of thirty or sixty
tents, under their different Sheiks. Horses were
picketed before every tent; camels were kneeling in
rows, or straggling in search of stray vegetation, or
browsing on the shoots of the stunted absinth and
thorny shrubs that studded the plain. As the band
approached this city of tents, the Arabs were at their
morning prayers, and the sound of the chant, from
such a multitude of voices, had an imposing effect, as
it rose in the distance. By the time they arrived, all

had betaken themselves to their occupations, some
driving their flocks to pasture, some tending their
horses—few giving more than a passing glance and a
" Salamo Allikoom," to the advancing party. It was
a strange contrast to the scene presented by the en-
campments of the Moorish soldiery;—there, all is confusion, and nothing heard from morn till night but
music, singing, and revelling, mingled with the constant discharge of fire-arms. *Here*, all was order, their
tents being their homes ; every one had his occupation,
while in and around the tents the women were employed grinding corn, spinning wool, weaving hayks in
hand-looms, &c. It is the difference between a tent
as a home, and a tent as an amusement. In the
midst of the camp were pitched the tents of the Chief,
marked by a large green silk banner; they were placed
in two concentric circles, the inner one entirely private.
In the outer circle, one large tent towards the East, and
the only one that opened outwards, was set apart for
audiences, for guests, for meeting the Sheiks on business, and disposing of disputes and causes among his
people. The dialect of Arabic, spoken in the desert, is
remarkable for its deep guttural intonation; that of
Marocco for its softness.

Sidi Hamed Ibn Ishem was sitting in this large
tent, which was only furnished with a few mat cushions,
but spread with carpets, when Ali and his band arrived. He wore the same dress as his people, his patri-
archal authority requiring no external mark of dis-
tinction. He was a fine model of masculine beauty,

tall and symmetrically made, but spare, and with femi-
nine-looking hands and feet. His hair clustered round
his head in short, glossy curls, and his whiskers and
moustache terminated in a short, wavy beard. His
features were aquiline; his head not large, but would
have served as a model for an Æneas. His countenance
and eye showed firmness and severity tempered by
benevolence and generosity, which commanded confidence and inspired sympathy. He was surrounded
by the principal Sheiks, when Ali halted his men, and
went in to make his report. The Sheik rose, and their
salutation was as of two friends and equals, kissing
each other's hands and heads.

"Welcome, O Sheik! Is all well?"

"God has blessed us, Ya Sidi; all is well!"

"Praise be to Him! Why does the Sheik ride
another horse? Where is Gazelle? You would not
part with him alive?"

"My lord has said:—he lies low on the Sahel.
The vulture and hyena are feasting on my beautiful,
he fell not unavenged, the hand that smote him lies
cold by his side on the plain: God's will be done!
Must not death come to all?"

"My heart is straitened for your loss: is it not
that of a friend? It was written, O Sheik! But
what—are there not horses in our tents? We will
find you another."

"May God enlarge my lord's tent, who soothes the
wounds of his servants as with the balm of Mecca.
This makes me not feel my loss."

"Are we not friends? Are we not brothers, children of Ishmael? What is mine is my brother's."

The business of the caravan having been disposed of, Ali informed him that a Jew had been taken travelling with the Cafila, and was waiting without to be introduced, he had not been injured, as he held a token from the Chief, and claimed his protection. Dismissing his companions, the Chief retired to a private tent, where Yusuf was conducted to his presence. And the son of Isaac bowed down and kissed the earth before the son of Ishmael, the lord of the desert.

"In the name of God, peace; and his blessing upon my lord, the Sheik, and upon his tents."

"Peace, O my friend!" said the Sheik, in a tone of encouragement. "Speak; you are fasting and fatigued. Speak—are we not alone?"

"The journey I have travelled to see my lord's face has been long, but it did not make me faint; thy servant is crushed with the sorrow that has preyed on his heart. Does my lord remember his servant Rabbi Shallum?"

"Can I forget him? God has taken him. Behold that horse," pointing to a noble black charger, picketed in front of the tent. "Did he not ransom his sire? and did he not aid me to escape from the hands of my enemies? and shall I not remember him? Has any evil befallen his house?"

"Alas! my lord, that is my errand: and that I speak truth, behold the token my lord gave into his hands. The hour of need is come."

And he presented the pouch, which the Sheik immediately recognised. Yusuf then related the history of Azora's arrest and danger, and that he had since heard that she had been removed to the Sultan's hareem. "And now, O my lord," he said, "if you will assist the child of your friend, her peril is pressing, and delay is death."

"Have I not given a pledge? and shall it not be redeemed? If it is in the power of my hand, she shall not perish, if it please God. This shall be attended to before all. Go now and refresh thyself. We will speak on this matter."

Yusuf hesitated in doubt. "O my lord, forgive my speech. God be praised for your promise of help. But doubts arise in my mind. We are Jews — we are despised, my lord is of a high race, and of a great heart; but will his servants among the tribes approve of his assisting us; and may not policy compel my lord to disappoint our hopes? Let not my words offend."

"You are forgiven: for thus do the people of the city act. But know that an Arab's Pledge is irrevocable. Who," said he, rising, while his face beamed with generous feeling, "who was it that rescued me and returned my father's son to his tents?—A Hebrew! Who restored the chief to his people?—A Hebrew! Who ransomed thy sire, my noble steed, from the galling yoke of an hireling?—A Hebrew! And who saved me from death, and from loss of liberty worse than death, and gave me once more to see the dark tents of my tribe, and to feel my heart again expand in the freedom of my dear native plains? All this weight of benefit was conferred on me by a Hebrew! Did he allow me to perish because I was of another faith? Did he forsake me in peril because I was a Moslem? No! We had this faith in common,—God is the God of nations. Let every man cleave to his own form that he has received from his fathers; but do good to all, like God's rain; and never abandon a son of Adam in distress, because he worships his God in a different manner from himself. And shall the Arab be shamed by the Hebrew? Shall Hamed Ibn Ishem remain in quiet enjoyment of all that the Hebrew's hand has restored, whilst his child lies in peril, and not arise to save her? Go, my friend, our tents are yours. Think better of the son of Ishem, and believe that he never gave a pledge, which, with the help of God, he will not, at whatever peril, to the uttermost redeem."

Yusuf, though his habits and pursuits had given him a practical turn of mind, could not help gazing with admiration at the noble form before him, draped in his falling hayk, his action giving emphasis to his generous speech; and he thought that such a man might have been Abraham, when greeting the angels at the door of his tent.

"May the blessing of the God of our father Abraham be upon you!" said he; and kissing the Sheik's hand he retired to the tent allotted to him, to rest after his long fatigues, and offer up his thanksgiving for the success of his mission.

Ali having disposed of the booty of the Cafila, repaired to his own camp.

"God be praised for your return," said his wife, who flew to embrace him, "how often are you absent now, O my lord, and I am left desolate in the tent!"

She was a type of Arab loveliness, was Zaïda; the bright crimson shone through her tinted, but transparent cheeks, her hair fell, a waving veil, over her shoulders, and her large eyes were turned inquiringly in his face. He returned her embrace, and then releasing himself from her soft arms, he sat down sorrowfully on the carpet, and threw down the soldier's belt.

"It is the will of God," he said; "there is gold, accursed be it, it has cost me my friend—Gazelle is dead!"

"Dead!" echoed Zaïda, and the beautiful creature again threw herself into her husband's arms, and wept on his bosom; she grieved for his loss, she grieved for her own; but she grieved more for what he had suffered. Her grief gave a new turn to his thoughts.

"Be consoled, my darling," he said, caressing her, and wiping away her tears. "God has given and God has taken; but have I not you? Have I not many blessings? Why do I complain? The gold will buy another horse; but—it will be another. Where is my boy? Where is Ishmael?"

"He went out early," she said, "but his return cannot be delayed: I see him coming even now."

A fine lad of twelve or fourteen now came up, holding a gun in one hand, and with the other leading a large tawny greyhound, whose sedate physiognomy contrasted with the bright, joyous face of the young Arab, as he ran to meet his father. He paused a minute as he passed the spot where the soldier's horse was tethered, and then embraced his father.

"My heart is joyful that you have returned in peace," said he, "but —" and he turned an inquiring and pained look towards the place whence he missed his loved companion.

"Yes, my boy," said Ali, "a stranger stands in the place of your friend, you will see Gazelle no more—he fell in a fray by the hand of an enemy."

"Gone for ever!" cried Ishmael: large tears rose to his eyes, which he could not control, and dashing down the stock of his gun, with childish wrath: "would that I had here the base-born that did the deed, even this tent should not protect him from vengeance!"

"Be silent, boy! you know not what you say. You are young. But learn that the sanctuary of this tent should protect even the murderer of thy father! But here, put away these things," giving him his sword, gun, and accoutrements.

Ishmael felt the justice of his father's reproof; but his young mind thought it a great hardship to forego a just revenge. Having put away the arms in a corner of the tent, he and his father joined in the meal which had been waiting, and was now sent out from the inner tent. By the time they had finished, an Arab was seen approaching, leading a fine iron-grey horse, completely equipped, and they went out to meet him.

" Sidi Hamed," said the Arab, " has sent you this horse to replace the one you have lost, and my lord desires you to be in readiness to mount in a few hours for a long journey."

" Tell the Sheik," said Ali, " that I am grateful for his gift. Is not my life at his service? Say I will await his orders."

The horse having been consigned to an attendant. " Go," said he to his son, " and tell your mother what you have heard—I cannot ! "

CHAPTER VIII.

THE SULTAN.

N the day succeeding the hunting party, the Sultan, having taken his place in his audience-hall, with his secretaries and officials in attendance, directed Abd el Aziz to have the executioners in readiness; and then ordered Abdslem to be brought before him. He was accordingly brought in heavily ironed, from the prison where he had lain all night. The pain from the treatment his hands had undergone was becoming excruciating; but he forced his features to assume an expression of composure; which was undisturbed by the preparations he saw making by the executioner as he passed; and on which he depended for his success in escaping from punishment. As soon as he had been forced to bow down before the Sultan, and was allowed to stand, and before waiting for the usual permission to speak : " May our lord's life be prolonged. Is this," said he, lifting up his tortured hands in chains, " is this the reward of loyalty ? Shall the breath of private slander deprive my lord of his most devoted slaves ? Where are my accusers ? What is my crime ?" and he looked boldly round on the audience.

The Sultan being in possession of such glaring

evidence of his guilt, was somewhat astonished at his assurance. "What mockery is this?" said he. "Is the slave mad? Read out this letter, that he and all may know that he dies with justice."

The Taleb, to whom the letter had been handed, opened the scroll, and read as follows:—

"In the name of the One God, the Merciful, peace and his blessing. To our friend Sidi Abdslem Ibn el Hadj, Marockshee. We have received and considered the words that you have sent us, requiring money to seduce the soldiers of your master the Sultan; time shall not be prolonged before you will be met by a faithful messenger: exert yourself, be faithful, and be assured of our friendship. Peace. This—day of Moharram, 1248." Attached was the seal of the Sheik of the Sebaïe.

A thrill ran through the assembly, as they listened to the perusal of this flagrant proof of guilt, and felt that his days were numbered. The Sultan had watched the prisoner's countenance, which did not appear to be disturbed by any conviction of guilt, but rather assumed an air of greater self-complacency.

"And is that, my lord," said he, "the crime that is laid to your slave's charge? Alas! for the dream of the seller of earthenware! On that letter I had built a vision of rewards and honours from the Khalifa, and behold what has befallen me! Let my lord slay me, if so it is written; but let my lord hear me alone—and your servant's innocence will be white, and my lord will hear matters of importance."

The Sultan was staggered; Abdslem had maintained his part with such coolness and confidence that the Sultan's curiosity was excited, though he never supposed he could explain away such convincing evidence. Fettered as he was he was harmless; and on a motion from the Sultan, the secretaries, officials, all, withdrew out of hearing, to the lower end of the hall, and Abdslem, kneeling at the border of the Sultan's carpet, on a motion to speak, proceeded as follows : —

"May my lord live for ever! It is now two months ago, that ever watchful to frustrate the designs of my lord's enemies, I noticed a trader, a man of suspicion, mixing with the soldiers; determined to know his object, I put myself in his way, and drew him into talk. I will not repeat his blasphemy against your highness, exalted of God; but pretending to be deceived, I lured him on, until he had the audacity to propose to me, on the part of an Arab Sheik, to corrupt my lord's servants from their allegiance, promising me rewards. I was immediately inspired with the design of entrapping the rebel Sheik, and placing him in my lord's power. I wrote a letter, to which that now read is an answer, and to ensure his coming, I asked for money, which he would either bring himself, or come with promises instead, for Arabs like not to part with their gold. The miscarriage of his letter has frustrated my plan, and, but for my lord's forbearance, must ere this have cost me my life. As it is, I have suffered; but it is in my lord's service. God is great! It was written."

This clever explanation of the affair, in which he

appeared to be so seriously compromised, had gradually changed the Sultan's feelings towards him ; but he remained for some minutes with his brows knit, his beard resting in his hand, and his eyes fixed on the prisoner's face, as though he would read his heart. " God is merciful," he said, at length. " This may be true, the All-knowing knows. Yes : you shall prove its truth. The Sheik will not know that his letter fell into our hands,—his messenger will come,—you will bring him before us Thus shall you prove your truth. You are free ! Guards there !" and half-a-dozen soldiers rushed in, expecting orders to drag Abdslem to his fate. " Knock off his fetters, and let his hands be released ; he is free !"

Abdslem prostrated himself and kissed the earth, he was then led out by the soldiers, invoking blessings on the Sultan's clemency.

The Wezeer and secretaries now resumed their seats.

" I have intelligence from Algiers, O my lord," said the Wezeer.

" Speak, O Hadjie," said the Sultan.

" There has been a battle near Oujda on our borders, and the Emir Abd el Kader has beaten the infidels."

" May the infidels be accursed !" said the Sultan.

" The Ameer has sent a white female slave for the Sultan's hareem."

" The slave will be welcome," said the Sultan.

" God is great !" said the Wezeer, " but as my

lord ean see, the object of the Ameer is to embroil the Sultan with the French, and compel us to be his allies."

"Are we Algerines and sons of Othman that we should fear the infidels?" said the Sultan; "send a letter of thanks to the Ameer, and a present of steeds with embroidered trappings."

"My lord's will shall be obeyed," said the Wezeer. He then continued, "The French are strong in ships, O Sultan! and Swerah will be attacked by sea, and where will be my lord's revenues from the merchants? Moreover, the slave is not young, and has grey eyes, and red hair: by the side of the houris of Mequinez, she is an Afreet!"

"Let her be sent back!" exclaimed the Sultan: "why should we quarrel with the Francese? They can stop our commerce on the sea. Who is Abd el Kader that we should fight for him? Is he not a Berebber of the Kabyles? Send orders, O Wezeer, to the Kaïd of Oujda to resist any violation of our frontier."

"The Khalifa shall be obeyed," said the astute Wezeer.

He then took up another letter. "Here, O my lord," he said, "is news that war is about to break out between the Inglees and the Oroose; may the Beneficent give us peace."

"O Wezeer," said the Sultan, "what is that to us? let the infidels fight, what is that to the true believers? if the dog bite the pig, or the pig bite the

dog, what is that to us? Are we not Moslemeen?"
And he arose and broke up the audience.

Azora sat alone in a room in the women's apartments; it was furnished with carpets, ottomans, and
cushions. At one end, a glass door opened into a
garden, full of fruit-trees and flowers, but surrounded
by high walls. An old woman to whose charge she
had been consigned had selected the room for her, and
treated her with every attention. Here, without al-
tering her dress, she had snatched an unrefreshing
sleep. She had received a communication from her
mother,—for gold can open a Sultan's hareem—en-
joining on her to gain time, by procrastination, to
further the measures taken for her deliverance, and
she naturally shrunk from hurrying on her own fate,
if delay might be obtained without a sacrifice of principle. Her eyes were fixed on the walls of her prison,
and she was absorbed in deep and painful thought on
her unfortunate position and probable fate, when she
was startled by the entrance of the Sultan. She immediately arose and stood by the door of the garden,
involuntarily, from fear or humility, removing as far as
possible from him.

"Have you an answer to my proposal, O light
of my earth?" said he, approaching her with a
smile.

"Alas, my lord!" said Azora, clasping her hands,
"is justice dead? is there no condition of freedom
but sinning against God, even the God of my fathers?"

G

"Talk not to me of gods," said he, impatiently;
"my religion does not interfere with my pleasure; if
it is to save you from danger, do not your priests
teach you that compulsion is not sin? But why, O
my beautiful, talk of sin?" he continued, in a winning
tone. "Is it a crime to love? Can your gentle eyes
spurn a Sultan from your feet? Drive me not to
despair. Oh, if you would but adopt our holy faith,
I, even I, would be your champion; and where would
be the slave that would dare to think a thought to
harm you? Oh, Azora! Azora! I have had no peace
since I saw you; you are the sultana, I am the slave,
—the victim. Oh, look on me at your feet, and have
pity,—on yourself, on me!" He was on his knee,
with his left hand he held her right, which was cold
as marble, while the other was stretched out implor-
ingly. There is no doubt he loved her, as much as
a man so incapable by habit of real love could do.
She was so different from the inmates of his hareem;
many of these doubtless had beauty, but it was the
difference of human beings reared in a torpid state of
seclusion, and one who had been always free!—the
fascination of intellect. Azora would not have been
woman, had she not been deeply moved by this earnest
appeal. To see him, before whom all men trembled,
a suppliant at her feet, it was a fearful trial for human
nature unaided. And she breathed an inward prayer
for help. She dreaded the storm which she saw
gathering, but felt more courage to brave his threats

than his entreaties. Gently disengaging herself from his hands, she said,—

"O my lord, tempt me not. Let not my lord kneel to his servant; threaten me, torture me, but let not my lord talk of love. Do I not know the fate of a favourite,—the plaything of a day; thrown by to pine in neglect and solitude? And shall I not expect, and deserve, worse than these,—I, a despised renegade, a traitoress to my faith, surrounded by jealous enemies,—and forsaken by my God? No!" said she firmly, and looking up to heaven, "rather let me die at once, than die a thousand deaths by dragging out a degraded life of shame and remorse, to end in eternal ruin."

And now the storm burst; his love spurned and his power braved, it is not easy to describe the tumult of passion, the more fierce from being seldom roused, that raged in the Sultan's breast, on•hearing this address. Love, revenge, fury, seized on him by turns, his emotions were too intense for utterance, but shown by the terrific working of his countenance; he bit his parched lip till the blood flowed, his eyes flashed fire, from under his dark stormy brow, and his frame trembled as if about to be overcome by a fit of insanity. While this hurricane lasted, the life of Azora, who stood terror-struck, hung by a frail thread. By a strong, effort he gradually recovered his self-possession, and when he spoke it was with frightful calmness; his face was deadly pale as he turned to depart, " This, then, is your decision ; you are prepared for the consequences ? "

In her resolve not to compromise her principles, Azora had forgotten the necessity of obtaining delay ; but having asserted these, she had now to risk the rectification of this omission.

" O my lord ! be not hasty," she said, " let me have time to consider ; perhaps — " but her voice faltered ; " but — if I must — die — a few days or weeks will be a short preparation for eternity ! "

The Sultan stopped, and fixed his eyes on her changing countenance, in which he thought he saw signs of her wavering, and his love prompted him to delay while any hope remained. He replied in his former calm tone, " Azora, I have granted your request ; two weeks shall you have for reflection. If at the end of that time you still spurn my love, by the tomb of the Prophet ! no power on earth shall save you."

· He was gone. Azora remained gazing at the closed door ; it was as a dream, the time had been so short which had transported her from her quiet home to be the inmate of a palace with her life in danger. Tears came to her relief, and she sought to realise her position ; she was not left long, however, to indulge her grief, for soon after the Sultan's departure, she was surrounded by the ladies of the hareem, who led her away to their own rooms ; and during the time that her fate was undecided, she was treated with the greatest kindness, attired in costly dresses, adorned with valuable jewels; and they endeavoured to amuse her with music and tale-tellers, leaving nothing untried to turn her from her purpose, and reduce her to their own state of captivity.

CHAPTER IX.

THE FALCON CAGED.

T was about eight days after the arrest of the Jewess that Hassan mounted his horse and rode out of the town by the south gate. He rode onwards, engrossed by his own bitter reflections, almost unconscious that the moon had risen and that he was now far from the city. At the time that he found his plans frustrated by Azora's appeal he was overcome by rage and disappointment; as these feelings subsided, his conscience upbraided him for his useless perjury, by which he had brought Azora into imminent peril without in the slightest degree promoting his own guilty plans; he was merely a jackal to a lion.

Having bitterly repented of his crime, his mind was now constantly haunted with the dread of the consequent death to Azora, with which he himself had threatened her. One image pictured on his mind seemed to have effaced and taken the place of all others. A beautiful figure, on a pyre, with the flames leaping around her, looked on him with a look of reproachful agony! Sleeping or waking it was the same, wherever he looked those sad eyes met his;

there was no escape; he was becoming a monomaniac. His life was lonely, the only other inmate of his home being a little orphan sister of five years old, to whom he was much attached, but who was hardly old enough as a companion to divert his mind; and at night he was quite alone.

He now dismounted and sat down on a bank, under the trees. The evening breeze brought to his ear the modulated murmurs of a neighbouring rivulet; they sounded to him as the moan of suffering. The moon poured her beams through the foliage of olive that overshadowed him, painting the ground with a tracery of waving leafage, that seemed to him as flames. The image faded for a time, as the silence of the night soothed his harassed mind, and he felt himself more immediately in the presence of God amid the calm scenes of nature. The lessons of childhood, and the principles of youth, which had not been wholly extinguished, rose up to accuse him; and overcome by shame and remorse, he leaned his head on his clasped hands and wept bitterly, until his heart was seared and his eyes were dry. Alas! man's tears harrow, but are no relief.

"Salemo Alikoom," said a clear voice near him; and remembering the lateness of the hour he started to his feet.

"And on you peace," he returned to the stranger, who now stood by his side. By the moonlight he could see that he was tall, with an aquiline nose, and short black beard, and dressed in the slovenly hayk and turban of a peasant. He had stopped to water his horse at the brook which flowed at a short distance, and Hassan was so absorbed in his reverie that he had approached him almost unperceived on the turf, and had been a partial witness to his emotion.

"Peace to the believer!" said the stranger; "you sit here so quietly enjoying the moonlight and the running water, that I suppose the town gates are shut for the night. This is a good place to camp under the sky, and we shall be better in each other's company. I am from Duquela, and not knowing the country, I have rather lost my way." Saying which he pulled a small carpet from his horse's saddle, and got out his hobbles to tie up his horse.

"Not so fast," said Hassan, won by his frank address, "I knew not it was so late; I do not sleep here when the town is so close. Certainly you must have lost your way, for Duquela is to the north. But are there not more ways of entering a town than by the gates?"

"By scaling the walls? You are a townsman, but if I were caught at that I might shorten my shadow, from which God preserve me!"

"God forbid!" said Hassan; "but I like you—promise secresy, and I will show you a way in; I discovered it by accident."

"On the faith of a Moslim," said Ali el Bezz, for it was he; and mounting their horses they rode on to the town. Ali had been despatched by the Chief, to Marocco, to watch over the safety of Azora, and to act as circumstances might require for her deliverance. He had received a minute description of the Moors, her accusers, from Yusuf, and he felt assured that one of them was now before him. This adventure promising him an entrance into the town without passing the gates, he saw at once would prove of immense advantage to him hereafter for purposes of escape. If he was not yet satisfied of his companion's identity, it was not long before he had evidence of the fact.

"What brings you to Marocco, O Moslim?" said Hassan as they rode side by side.

Ali fixed his eyes on his face, on which the moon shone, and answered indifferently,—

"I heard there was an infidel to be burnt for wishing to recant."

Hassan started, and turned round on the speaker, who had thus given a wrench to the weapon that rankled in his wounded spirit, and who appeared quite unconscious of the effect his words had produced as he continued,—

"We heard the news in our province, and I came to see the sight. It will be a grateful sacrifice to the Prophet. God is merciful! The Sultan is too indulgent to the infidels."

"Woe to thee, O Moslim!" said Hassan in an excited tone. "Think you the pangs and shrieks of a son of Adam in torture can be grateful to a merciful God? Think you the diabolical spirit of the murderers can be pleasing to a beneficent Creator? In the infancy of the faith the Prophet's policy allowed this;

now it is useless, barbarous! And this is a woman! O God! O God!" And he pressed his hands to his eyes as though the flames blasted them.

Ali gazed on him with unfeigned surprise; at first he thought he was counterplotting to mislead him, but sincerity was too plainly marked on his haggard face to admit of a doubt.

"From you, this!" he said; "is it possible? Even as the tongue of the Cadi is before, while his hand is behind for the bribe; so men act one thing and speak another."

"And who am I?" said Hassan; "and who is your father's son that you reflect on me as double-faced? When have we met before?"

"Never! and yet I am not wrong," said Ali, fixing on his face a stern and inquiring glance; "I am not wrong in thinking I speak to the accuser of this woman. Do I not speak to the principal cause of her sufferings and death? Hassan, son of Ibráhim, do I not know you?"

Hassan's blood rushed to his brow and then left his face ashy pale, as he said in a low voice,—

"Just God! is the brand of blood already on my brow that even strangers know the murderer? The guilt of innocent blood is even now beginning to fall on my head."

"You repent?" said Ali; "then why have you done nothing to save her?"

"Too late! Oh, that I could! But how do I know," said Hassan, checking himself, "that I am not trusting to an enemy? What matter? It is known! What have I to fear? I would give my life—a life that is hateful to me, if it would save hers. And you, —you have travelled far to see this scene of horror? —I see it now!"

"I spoke to gain your confidence," said Ali; "knowing you as the destroyer of the innocent, I was your foe; now,—we are friends, and I can trust you. But however little value you place upon your own life, when I entrust you with a secret which would be no less fatal to mine, you must swear to confide it to no other. I come to save her!"

"I swear by my father's head never to betray you," said Hassan; his spirit rising with the hope of being able to co-operate in any way towards undoing his evil work. "But how?"

"We shall find a way, if it please God," said Ali, "when the time comes. I have met you in a fortunate hour; I see by the leather thong that you wear that you belong to the Palace guards, this will give you the opportunity of letting the Jewess know that help is at hand. You must see her yourself or bribe some of the eunuchs or women. Tell her to seek delay, and profit by any occasion we may be able to devise to save her."

"I will do it," said Hassan; "at the risk of my life I will do it."

The plain around the city of Marocco is very dangerous to ride over at night, being intersected by long lines of pits, extending from the walls towards the mountains; these pits are connected with underground canals by which the town is watered; and these again are connected with each other by tunnels. The pits are twenty and thirty feet deep; and from their sides fig and other trees, and even date-palms, shoot up above the surface of the plain, while beneath is heard the rushing of the buried streams.

The horsemen were now obliged to follow each other cautiously in single file till they came to a fondak, or caravanserai, outside the town walls, near one of the closed gates. The keeper of this let them in, cursing to himself at being disturbed from his sleep. Within, all was silent except the creaking of the camels' teeth, as they lay ruminating and waving their gaunt necks in the moonlight; their drivers lay around rolled up in their hayks. After securing their horses they let themselves out. Hassan then led the way for about half-a-mile, until he stopped on the brink of one of the pits above described, and, telling his companion to follow cautiously, he lowered himself down through the branches of a spreading tree, and then, by holding on to roots and shrubs, came by an easy declivity to the bottom of the pit. Being joined by Ali, they found themselves in one of the tunnelled passages, in which there was merely a run of water; following this for some distance in a stooping posture, they came to a nearly dry well, which they ascended with ease by the projecting stones left in its sides, and emerged, through a thicket of tangled brambles and flowering shrubs, into the court-yard of a large aban-

doned building about a hundred feet square, surrounded
by colonnades of massive stone pillars.

Ali's quick eye was not slow in calculating the
advantages of such a mode of exit from a hostile town,
and he treasured every mark in his mind for future
use in case of need. Crossing a paved court, they
went out by an unfastened gate studded with iron nails,
and found themselves in an open space within the
town; here they separated; Ali being well acquainted
with the interior of the town; after arranging where
to meet each other, without the necessity of public
recognition. It happened that Ali had been very
unwisely intrusted by the Sheik with the money for
Abdslem; and this, as we shall see, was very nearly the
means of upsetting all their plans, and at the same
time of finishing the "Falcon's" career.

Abdslem was beginning to feel very impatient at
the delay of the Sheik's emissary, whom he was now
bent on betraying; to prove his assumed innocence, to
the Sultan. Although he had with consummate assurance blinded the Sultan to the evidence of his guilt,
this was wanting to restore his confidence, or ensure
his safety. On this night he was standing at his open
door, when he was accosted by a stranger muffled in
a woollen hayk. "Peace be to you! Is your name
Abdslem?"

"To you peace: my name is Abdslem! What
would you with him?"

"I would speak with him in private!"

"Bismallah! come into your servant's house."

Abdslem could scarcely conceal his triumph; as they went into the room he closed the door, and lighted a three-cornered tin lamp; before doing which he had composed his features, and then sat down opposite his visitor.

"Have you received a letter from him to whom you wrote?"

"I have, and by water: it was a device of cunning."

"I acknowledge the token; have you seen the bearer since? He did not return."

"No! I understand he went on a long journey; his head was deranged as it seemed. But if you are not satisfied, behold the letter!"

"It is enough, it is the Sheik's seal; meet me to-morrow at dusk at the palm-grove inside the Duquela gate, there you shall receive it; you know your work."

Notwithstanding Abdslem's eagerness to secure his prize, his examination of the powerful frame of the Arab showed him that he had not a chance against him single-handed, and to take any step that would inspire him with alarm would be to lose him altogether; he therefore resolved to wait, and make sure of him, as well as secure the money. "Inshallah," he said, "I will not fail you: will you not share a soldier's supper?"

"May his blessing be with you, and increase your store: better that we be not seen together. Peace."

"And to you peace," echoed Abdslem, as he closed the door after him, "for to-night—but to-morrow!—half a quintal of iron on *your* limbs shall partly avenge me for my sufferings."

He thought the next day would never pass, at length the evening wore on, and Abdslem having procured a dozen armed men from the Kaïd of the town, placed them in ambush close to the place of meeting; and anxiously awaited the arrival of Ali, who did not appear until it was quite dusk.

"This way," whispered Abdslem, drawing him into the date-grove. "Come more within the shade."

The feathery boughs above their heads sighed dismally in the night breeze, and one large columnar tree lay prostrate on the earth.

"Let us sit here: where is the money?"

"It is here," said Ali, producing the bag, the next minute he was startled by a movement amongst the bushes behind him, and, looking round, saw figures rising up in the dim light from their shelter.

"This for your treachery!" said he, dropping the bag, and making a blow at Abdslem with his dagger; but the other was on his guard, and avoided it by springing back, and Ali unfortunately stumbled over the fallen tree: the soldiers rushed upon him, and he was overpowered by numbers, disarmed and bound, whilst the traitor stood looking on with folded arms, congratulating himself on his success.

"Inshallah! you shall live to repent of this night's work," said Ali, "if it please God."

"Your days will not be long enough to see it," replied Abdslem, sneeringly.

"You will not be the first that Ali el Bezz has lived to be revenged on."

"What!" said Abdslem, "have I been so fortunate as to capture that notorious robber Ali el Bezz? God be praised."

"The day may not be so propitious to you as you suppose," said Ali: "'tis your turn to-day—but to-morrow—beware the 'Falcon's Swoop.'"

And Abdslem quailed before his prisoner, although bound and in his power; his triumph was also embittered by the dread of retribution, which, if Ali escaped, would inevitably fall on him, and even if he did not, would sooner or later overtake him at the hands of the Arab's family. Taking up the bag of money he accompanied the soldiers to the prison, and, after seeing Ali secured, returned to his own house intending to make his report to the Sultan in the morning.

CHAPTER X.

BLOOD FOR BLOOD.

ON the day that consigned Ali thus treache-
rously to a dungeon, a small knot of soldiers
were sitting at the Sultan's gate, performing
a combined attack on a huge pyramid of Ouscusoo,
into which they plunged their hands half-way to the
elbow, and swallowed the large balls of granulated
flour, which they squeezed up like snow in their
fingers, and it was not till they had nearly demolished
the mutton and fowls buried in this tumulus, that they
found time to use their tongues for any other purpose.

"Praise be to God!" said Omar, wiping his mouth
and shaking the grains from his beard. "Did you hear
the news from Algiers?"

"Here, Ombark, you slave, pour water on my
hands."

"We heard," said Mehedin, "that the town had
been retaken, and the infidels driven into the sea,—a
curse on their fathers!"

"May you ride three days on a thirsty camel! Why
do you believe such lies? though I would it were true,"
said Cassim.

"Listen to me, O Moslemeen," said Omar, with an

air of importance, "were not the infidels enticed into
the mountains by the Emir Abd-el-Kader? and when
they had passed the defile, did he not cut off their
retreat? Great was the slaughter of the infidels; a
price had been fixed for every head brought in, but it
had to be lowered and lowered or the Sultan's treasury
would not have paid for all; eight thousand were
slain!"

"To God the glory!" said Cassim; "but you,
Mahmoud, what say you to that, you, that think the
Nazarene dogs invincible?" Mahmoud was a young
man about twenty, of rather unprepossessing appearance, with small restless grey eyes, and a gentle and
rather feminine countenance.

"I did not say so," answered Mahmoud calmly;
"but I know from letters which are true, received by
the Weezeer, that the whole infidel army was but seven
thousand, of which more than six thousand returned to
Djezair. May they be exterminated!"

"The curse of the Prophet on your house," said
Cassim to Omar; "why do you invent such lies, and
why are we such fathers of the ears to believe them?"

"Know you to whom you speak?" returned Omar,
flushing with rage. "Tenfold curses on your father,
and may every dog's son of your tribe be destroyed!"

Cassim was of Arab family, and this was too much
for him.

"That from one dog," said he, and he hurled the
pitcher, from which he was washing his hands, at
Omar's head; but for his large turban, the blow

would have been more serious: as it was, he was
stunned; but recovering, sprung to his feet, dagger
in hand, vowing vengeance; but now the others inter-
fered to stop the quarrel, and Cassim, cooled by the
effect of his missile, regretted his hastiness. Mahmoud was particularly zealous in pacifying the sufferer.

"Shall I not drink the coward's blood?" said
Omar, struggling with Mahmoud, who was forcing
him to sheath his dagger.

"What will you gain by that, or by eating him
too? Curse the devil, and be friends; of all things I
hate a revengeful temper; he is sorry for it."

"Who can stand such treatment?" said Omar,
trying to swallow his rage. Eventually, after several
relapses, the quarrel was made up, and the two were
kissing each other's heads, in token of forgiveness,
when they were joined by Abd-el-Aziz.

"I have just been told," said he, "that the Cafila
to Timbuctoo has been plundered in the Beled-el-
Jerede by the Woled Abu Sebah, and some of the
people killed. I hope, Mahmoud, that your brother
Mohammed did not go with them; it was said that he
did."

Mahmoud turned deadly pale.

"Where had you this news?" said he, rising, "for
I must know the truth."

"The person who told me was the old Fez merchant in the Caseria; he was one of them, and has lost
all his goods."

Mahmoud hastily departed.

" Poor youth ! if his brother be killed, woe to him ; his life will be darkened, for he loved him exceedingly."

The love which existed between these two brothers was known to them all; they had been together from childhood; the quiet, unassuming disposition of the younger accorded well with the somewhat wild and bragging character of his brother, and his retiring habits preventing him mixing much with others of his station, made him cleave with more affectionate dependence to his brother; he had endeavoured to dissuade him from this journey, but his love of enterprise had prevailed. And now, with a fearful dread that they were parted for ever, Mahmoud made his way with rapid steps towards the Caseria, through long streets of shops, shaded from the sun by date-boughs supported by poles thrown across the street from wall to wall, hustling his way through crowds of people, water-carriers, sweetmeat-sellers, Dellals hawking their goods, camels, mules, and horses, until, overcome with heat and fatigue, he reached the bazaar, where shops, packed with shawls, scarfs, silk handkerchiefs, and European goods, invited the purchaser. Here he was informed that the object of his search had gone to the fondak. The story of the plunder of the caravan was in every one's mouth. Resting a minute to take a draught of water to moisten his parched lips, and which the water-carrier, with his usual "Allaw Kerim!" emitted from the neck of a goatskin gathered in his hand, into a brass bowl: Mahmoud set off on another

long round, and at length found the Fez merchant
sitting in one of the empty partitions of the colonnade,
round the courtyard of the fondak.   His face was
woe-begone, and his fingers as usual combed his grey
beard, as he ruminated over his losses, when he was
addressed by Mahmoud,—

"Salamo Alikoom; Sidi Idries! were you with the
Cafila that was plundered in the Desert?"

"Woe unto me!—who else?" said the little man
with a groan, and then began, half to himself, enu-
merating his losses: "Were there not three bales of
silk, worth six hundred dollars, five camel-loads of
grocery and spice, four hundred and fifty dollars at
least, not to count expenses and camel hire. Woe is
me, to leave my own shop, to be ruined in my old age,
besides this there were two ——"

"Then you can inform me—" interposed Mahmoud,
impatiently.

"Is it not I that can give you information of the
whole affair?   Have I not paid dearly for experience?
As I was saying, — Two bales of cowries, upwards of
140,000, one hundred and forty dollars."

"But what I want to ask you—" said Mahmoud,
beginning to lose all patience.

"Little by little, my friend," said Sidi Idries, "and
I will tell you all; little by little the camel gets into
the saucepan. To think of the slaves, and the gold-
dust, and the ivory, I have lost. Our lives were
saved — yes — God is merciful — but what is life
without the means of living — the sum total ——"

Mahmoud's patience here gave way —

"For God's sake, hear me!" thundered he, striking his clenched hand on the shopboard, and putting a sudden stop to the merchant's volubility. "I wish to know if any of your company were killed by the Arabs? It is not from curiosity, but my brother went with them, and has not returned : I fear some evil has befallen him."

His earnest and excited manner had driven the old man's losses from his head for the present, and he told him that he had reason to believe that one of the soldiers of their party had lost his life; and his description of his appearance left no doubt on Mahmoud's mind that it was his brother. His head swam, and a faintness at his heart made him reach to the doorway for support, and he sank on the shop-sill, the sweat streaming down his face. The old merchant was moved nearly to tears at witnessing his suffering.

"It is the will of God, O my son!" he said; "have patience : was it not written?"

"There is more written, O my father," said he; "there is vengeance!" and he wiped the cold sweat from his brow; "but tell me everything — tell me all!"

The merchant then told him, that after they were plundered and stripped, an Arab, who had gone in pursuit of the soldiers, had returned with a soldier's horse instead of his own, and carrying his clothes and arms; and that when they started on their return they had passed the body·of a horse and man, lying on the plain in the moonlight, with a flock of vultures gorged and slumbering at a little distance, until daylight should enable them to renew their feast.

"Now I remember," he said, "the soldier's name was Mohammed."

Mahmoud's worst fears were confirmed.

"Is it known who the Arab was?" he inquired, with a quivering voice.

"Arabs are like dates," said the merchant, " one like another; but this one was not of the flock; he gave us his name himself; he was the famous Ali-el-Bezz!"

"I have heard it before," said Mahmoud, as he turned slowly away to dream of vengeance; "but now it is written here"— and he struck his brow—"in fire!"

He returned to his home, and though he wept in private the loss of his brother, he subdued his emotion, when he was obliged to repair to the Palace-guard, and appear among his comrades; but he sat abstracted and taciturn, torturing his brain with plans of vengeance. If Ali had been living in the town, he would have slain him by treachery, or hired assassins; any means seemed excusable to compass his revenge; but how reach him in the Desert; and who would aid him against so redoubtable a foe, who was supposed to possess a charmed life? He felt at last reduced to the painful necessity of waiting until his enemy should venture to the town, when he resolved to hunt him down at any risk. He little knew at the time that his revenge was brought to his own door, and he had only to arise and strike.

His comrades, knowing the cause of his melancholy, forbore to intrude on him. They had just finished their supper, and were preparing to set the watch for the night, when Abdslem joined them. He was in high spirits, and exhibited a handsome embroidered silk scarf, which he unwound from his head, for their admiration.

"Look at this," he said; "I received it this morning from the Sultan's own hands; may he be exalted; I told you I should not be long in disgrace."

"It is beautiful," said Mehedin, while it passed round; "but what great thing have you done to merit it?"

"Not a small exploit. Did I not seize an Arab spy with my own hand; and who do you think he turned out to be? Why, no other than that dare-devil Sheik, Ali-el-Bezz!" and Abdslem twirled the scarf round his head in a handsome turban above his ugly face.

Mahmoud, who had at first paid little attention to the speaker, sprang forward at the electrical sound of that name.

"Who?" he said; "repeat that name," laying his hand on Abdslem's shoulder, while his features worked, his eyes glared, and his whole frame trembled.

Abdslem looked at him, half doubting his sanity.

"I tell you," he repeated, "I have seized the notorious robber Ali-el-Bezz; and he is now as safely lodged as walls and chains can keep him."

"Thanks be to God!" exclaimed Mahmoud, grinding his teeth, and raising his clenched hands, while a satanic smile overspread his countenance; "he is in my power; my revenge is sure!" and gathering up his cloak, he rushed out of the gate.

As he came into the street the moon threw her pale light on his haggard face, and reminded him that it was now too late to take further steps that night. He returned to his own house, and threw himself on his mattress, but sleep came not to the relief of his fevered frame; and his heated brain pictured to him his murdered brother, pale and bleeding, reproaching him for his delay.

The dogma of the Koran, which in practice is the Moorish law, is "eye for eye," "tooth for tooth," "life for life;" if the offence is proved, the Sultan himself hardly dares to refuse retaliation on the wrongdoer, and if the accuser perseveres in demanding justice, he must deliver up the accused to his vengeance.

Before the day dawned, Mahmoud was sitting at the inner gate of the palace, waiting impatiently till the Sultan should ride forth to the audience-hall (M'shouar); and when after several long hours he came out, surrounded by his guards and attendants, there was heard a voice clear above the noise of the cavalcade,—

" Justice! O my lord! Justice! Blood for blood!"

The Sultan ordered the speaker to be brought before him, asked him the reason of his complaint, and whom he accused.

" My lord, I accuse Ali-el-Bezz," said Mahmoud; " he is now in prison, and I demand his life for the life of my brother, whom he has murdered."

" How know you that he hath done this?" said the Sultan, " we must have proof."

" The witnesses are all those who have returned from the plunder of the Cafila."

." We will inquire further into this matter," said the Sultan, "and if we find that your charge is true, we may not deny you justice."

Then giving the necessary orders, he rode on, leaving Mahmoud, to whom every hour of suspense seemed an age, sitting at the gates to await his return. It was midday, and he was still at his station; no food had passed his lips, and the call of the crier from the Mosque had rolled over him unheard, but as soon as the Sultan re-entered, the same clear voice rung in his ears,—

" Justice! my lord! Justice! Blood for blood!"

The Sultan made a gesture of impatience. From the inquiries he had caused to be made, he found that the charge was true; but as the Arab had been taken in a political intrigue, he wished to spare his life for the present, with the view of obtaining information from him, and making use of him for his own service.

" Bring him before us;" and Mahmoud advanced.

"What sum would pay for this?" said the Sultan. "We would compromise this matter; of more use to you will be the fine of redemption than the death of the Arab: this cannot restore your brother, it was written."

Mahmoud's lip curled, and his eye glistened, "My lord's will is his slave's," he said, "and the will of the Khalifa of the Prophet will not wish to swerve from the Prophet's law. Shall I sell my brother's blood? If," said he, with fierce energy, "for every drop of the Arab's base blood, you offered me your hands full of gold, it should be as dross. No! not for his weight in diamonds would I forego my just revenge, or lose the satisfaction of witnessing the last groan issue from the gasping soul of my brother's murderer!"

From the intense vindictiveness of his spirit, the Sultan saw that it would be useless to combat his resolve; and as he was not very intent on saving Ali; within a few hours Mahmoud received the order to the keeper of the prison, directing him to deliver Ali up to him for execution.

His delight at receiving this order amounted to rapture; he kissed the Sultan's seal affixed to it, and placed it next his heart, as though it had been a token from his beloved; clasping it there he hurried to his house, dreading lest anything should occur to change the Sultan's mind, and intervene between him and his revenge. Arrived at home, he slung on his powder-horn and bullet-pouch, and taking his gun, which his impatience did not permit him to load, he hastened to the public prison.

Hassan on leaving his companion had proceded to fulfil his promise of warning Azora. Ali was right in supposing him well acquainted with the topography of the palace, from his position; and he was, moreover, intimate with many of the attendants of the household. He first provided himself with a bottle of the strong spirit which the Jews distil from raisins, put on a dark coloured dress, and then set off for the palace. Avoiding the main entrance, he skirted the walls till he came to a small side door, here he rolled a stone in a handkerchief, and gave five muffled knocks; after a short pause, the door opened of itself, the latch being raised by a string from above; he entered in the dark, and ascending a narrow stair in the thickness of the wall, entered a small square chamber lighted by a brass lamp; here on a carpet sat one of the Sultan's chief eunuchs; he had a flabby face, a heavy eye, and was very corpulent; his dress was of fine materials, and he wore an enormous white turban on his head; a bristle grew here and there on his chin.

"How is uncle Mobarik?" said Hassan, after the usual salutes.

"Well, O cheerer of my heart," said Mobarik. "how long it is since I have seen the son of my uncle!"

"I had work, O my friend, and could not come."

"Oh, we have heard. Allaw Ackbar. Work, yes, we have heard."

"And then, O my uncle, I like not to come empty-handed, and it is so difficult now to pass the stuff through the gate of the Jews' town; but there," producing the bottle, "is some true water of life; the Sultan does not drink better. None of your fig or date brandy, but distilled from grapes, and flavoured with anise : try it."

"Is it lawful, O light of my eyes?" said Mobarik, while his own eyes twinkled as he poured out half a tumbler full.

"Is it not lawful?" said Hassan.

"The Koran forbids it," said Mobarik.

"The Koran does not forbid it," said Hassan; "am I not a taleb? Hear the Koran ! Thus it is written— 'Intoxicating drink is created for man, but the harm of it is greater than its benefit; therefore, O Moslem, forbear.'" Mobarik had drained his glass before the quotation was finished. "And," continued Hassan, "the great commentator, Kumalodeen, interprets this, 'To those who can drink in moderation and without harm, it is permitted—to others, not.'"

"Truly, thou art a lawyer, and wisdom cometh out of thy mouth ; doth it not warm the stomach and cheer the heart?"

When Mobarik had finished about half the bottle to his own share, Hassan only helping him for form's sake, his ashy-brown face had acquired a sort of glow, and he seemed in the happiest temper for Hassan's purpose. It was no easy task for him to talk slightingly of what caused him such intense pain, but he forced himself to bear it.

"So you have heard," said he, "of Hassan converting the infidel?"

"Oh, yes!" said Mobarik, taking off his turban, and with a comical leer on his face; "the hawk struck the quail, and the eagle bore it off."

"God is great! There is more game a-field," said Hassan; "but how heard you the affair?"

"Is not the infidel in my ward?" said Mobarik.

"Then she is in the garden room," said Hassan; "that is all right."

"What garden room? and what is right?" said Mobarik, whose professional vigilance was awakened.

"Hast thou forgotten, O fat man! the carpenter's lad that was taken in to repair the door-lock?"

Before he could say more, Mobarik had closed his mouth with his hand,—

"Wilt thou be silent, O unfortunate? If thou didst escape, thank God; art thou weary of thy life?"

"Perhaps I am," said Hassan, "but thou wert well paid for that affair;" and he slapped the pocket of his caftan, making the money that it contained ring. "Now, uncle Mobarik, put on your turban, and listen to me. Shall I put you in the way of pocketing a nice little sum of fifty dollars?" The flabby face grinned. "Good! I must see this Jewess." The

mouth fell open, the eyes rounded, and with his turban
stuck on awry, any one less heavy at heart than Hassan
must have been convulsed with laughter. His mouth
then closed tight, and his head shook from side to
side.

"Am I an Afreet of fifty lives," said he, "that I
should tamper with the Sultan's hareem?"

"Mobarik, you are a father of the ears, any one
may see a Jewess. Hareem indeed! if it had been a
Mooress, there would be danger, besides, it is only a
letter; see, you would not lose fifty dollars?"

"Give me the money; I will give her the letter."

"Do you see my horns growing, O wise one? Or
have I been eating dates till the honey runs out of my
eyes? Do pillared dollars grow on trees, that you
have only to raise your hand and pick? Now, take
another glass, and listen to what I say. I have been
offered one hundred dollars, to give a letter into the
infidel's own hand. I refused, unless I knew the contents; it was read to me, for it is in the Hebrew
character—see, it is open. In it, they beg her to
submit to her fate, as all they have done to obtain her
liberty has been without success, and it is better for
her to be a Moslem than lose her life. I took the
money, and promised, as I knew you would not refuse
to help me."

"Then you were mistaken," said Mobarik, sulkily,
"I will not risk my head."

Hassan looked at him steadily for a minute, "I
swear by Allah, that *you* shall help me, and that I

will not leave until I have seen the Jewess; and now I
will show you that it is safer, and more profitable for
you to consent, than to refuse; look at me, I am a
stronger man than you, would it not be easy to me, O
my uncle, to bind you, and go without your leave? I
know the way, you would not dare to give an alarm,
for my being in here, and your friend there in the
bottle, would be sufficient to cost you the skin of your
back, and perhaps your head. But what is there to prevent my killing you," he continued, advancing towards
him with his hand on his dagger—"we are alone—but
for our old friendship?"

Mobarik had shrunk into the corner, in real alarm,
his face having again assumed its ashy hue: "Let us
be friends," said he, "give me the money: have you
not sworn that I shall help you, and an oath must be
kept?"

"Yes!" said Hassan, "and then it is a good action
to persuade the Jewess to her conversion. I will stay but
the time for an answer to the letter: go on before to see
that all is safe."

Mobarik having received the money, led the way
down-stairs, crossed a court-yard, and unlocking a side
door, admitted Hassan, directing him to lock the door
on his return, for which purpose he left the key in the
lock. Hassan found himself amongst the fruit trees,
with which the interior court was thickly planted; and
under their shadow, he made his way towards a light
which shone out through a glass door, at a little distance and which was half-open.

Azora was reclining on the cushions, one hand supporting her head, while the other rested on a small Hebrew Bible, which lay open before her. A large brass lamp, on an embossed pillar, stood on the carpet, and threw its light on her sweet, calm face. She was so deeply absorbed that she did not notice the entrance of Hassan, whose tread was dulled by the soft carpet, and he stood gazing, with clasped hands, on that face so pale and yet so peaceful; and though his affection for her was revived, it was in a hallowed form, and his heart smote him for the part he had taken in bringing one so good and so beautiful into her present peril. A deep-drawn sigh aroused her from her meditations, and made her aware of his presence. In her present position, her mind was not in a state to be startled by such a circumstance; her first feeling was surprise, and the next the fear of the consequences to himself. She felt resigned to her fate, and no feelings of ill-will could harbour in her bosom.

"Hassan," she said, rising, "am I not free from your presence even here?"

"No!" said he, "that time is past, but repentance has come too late to undo what has been done."

"God be praised!" interrupted Azora, "but know you your peril if found here? Fly! lest you also fall a victim."

"She is of the angels," muttered Hassan. "I am in her power, a word would avenge her, yet she only thinks of my danger; I, the cause of her death. Yes, I, her murderer. Oh, my brain! Allah, have mercy!

I

That I take this risk," he continued, addressing her, "is a proof that I now speak truth. I am sent to warn you that you have friends, who are working for and watching over your safety; you also must watch every opportunity, and profit by it. The Sheik of the Sebäie, who gave a pledge of protection to your father, has vowed to save you. I know not what threats or torture may be intended by the tyrant; but be sure that in the hour of danger friends will be near, and may God deliver you. Here is a token you must remember." And he gave her a slip of paper, with a few Hebrew words upon it.

"It is well," said Azora; "if God has raised me up friends, may He prosper their endeavours; if they fail, God's will be done! But haste—save yourself!"

Hassan was turning to depart, but stopped and said, with a trembling voice,—

"Oh, Azora! though torment wait me, I *cannot* go till you have granted one request."

"I, what is there in *my* power to grant? I, a captive!"

"Oh, much, much!" and he fell on his knees, and raised his hands in supplication. "Forgiveness!—I ask —forgiveness for the wrong I have done you, and—O God!—what may yet be—may He avert it. Can you, oh, can you forgive me?"

"Can I forgive you?" she repeated, raising her eyes to heaven with a smile, "as I hope for pardon from Him before whose throne I must ere long appear —from my soul I forgive you! But fly! I hear sounds approaching!"

A scalding tear fell on her hand, as Hassan pressed it to his lips, and then, disappearing through the door-way, he retraced his steps, locked the gate of the garden, and rejoined Mobarik, who was anxiously waiting to let him out.

"I have the answer," he said; "may your sleep be blessed. When shall we have another bottle of keef?"

"When I carry pebbles and eggs in the same bag, O son of my uncle," replied Mobarik, as he closed the door after him.

Soon after he had left, the female attendants summoned Azora to retire for the night; before which, she had looked at the paper left with her by Hassan, it contained only these words, "The black horse."

It was the next day that Hassan heard with the greatest dismay of the seizure of Ali-el-Bezz, which threatened to frustrate all attempts for the Jewess's safety. In the Moorish prisons the principal reliance is placed on the heavy chains with which they are shackled for the safe keeping of prisoners, the rooms being inefficient, and the guards careless; the shackles are riveted on the arms and legs by a smith, and the chains terminate in a massive ring in the wall. Hassan, as one of the Sultan's guards, knew that he would have no difficulty in communicating with the prisoner without suspicion; and the first thing he did before repairing thither was to purchase a large triangular file, which he concealed in his waist-belt. As soon as Ali had been secured as described above, he sat down on a stone, the only furniture of the cell, overcome with shame and vexation at allowing himself to be so entrapped. When this passed, his mind turned to other and more tormenting thoughts. The vision of his black tent on the Desert rose painfully to his imagination; he saw his wife looking out for his return, and all the trifling, but to him important details associated with his home, gave poignancy to his suffering; he sprang to his feet, only to be reminded by the irons on his limbs that he was no longer free !

He sat down and endeavoured to compose himself to think over his chances of escape; he examined his chains and their connexion with the wall, and was forced to the conclusion that unaided there was no hope ! It was early in the morning when he heard a voice, which he recognised, outside the iron-barred window of his cell, and his heart bounded with hope.

"These poor devils of prisoners would be starved but for the charity of the Moslem. I will begin this morning with a good action, and spend half a peçeta on them. O thou son of evil fortune !" said Hassan, coming to the grating, "take the alms of the Moslem, for the love of God." (And in a lower voice, "Cut the links next to your arms and legs.") "I am poor, O my brother, or I would give thee more. (You can overpower and gag the keeper of the prison.) Pray to the Saint Sidi Abd-el-Kader for me. (Your horse will be in waiting where we parted yesterday.) God give you a safe deliverance !"

He then sauntered away, while Ali, overjoyed, set to work to free himself from his chains, which, allowing for the interruptions he would be subject to by the coming in and out of the keeper, he expected to accomplish by noon. The links were made of soft iron, about ten inches long each, the rod of which they were forged being three inches in circumference; he found, after cutting through one, that by an exertion of strength, using his hands and feet, he could force it open and release the shackle; he had disengaged himself from three of his chains, and had cut through the remaining one on his left leg, which only required to be forced open; his heart already beat high, with the anticipation of liberty, when he was again disturbed by the approach of the keeper. Concealing the ends of his chains in his hayk, he huddled down by the wall, looking sulky, until he should leave as usual. This time, however, the keeper brought with him a stranger.

"Be it known unto thee, O enemy of God!" said the keeper, "that thou art convicted of the murder of a Moslem named Mohammed. And know further, that his brother, named Mahmoud, has claimed thy life for the life of his brother, according to the law, and has brought an order from the Sultan (may his throne be exalted!) to deliver thee unto him."

He then turned and left the room, the door of which he closed after him; and the avenger of blood and his victim were left together.

Ali at once saw the extent of his danger, and that, if he failed to liberate himself from the remaining chain, his life was ended. Luckily for him Mahmoud

had brought his gun unloaded; and as he was in no
hurry, now that he seemed sure of his prey, the delay
would give Ali the opportunity of making an effort to
disengage himself from the chain.   Revenge, like all
fierce pleasures, is chiefly delightful in anticipation.
Imagination exaggerating the enjoyment it promises,
these feelings gradually die away as the time for action
approaches; for if the excitement increased in pro-
portion up to that point, the overstrained mind would
render the body powerless to carry its plans into
practice with firmness and success.   Mahmoud was
disappointed; he fixed his gaze on his victim expecting
to see him quail with dread; he came to luxuriate in
his fears, and gloat over his despair as he begged
his forfeit life, and he anticipated the delight, when
he begged for mercy, of planting the death-shot
in his shrinking heart.   But Ali returned his gaze
undaunted, and he felt that his vengeance was in-
complete.

He began charging his gun; his voice trembled
with rage as he said,—

"O dog! you do not fear death? We shall
see. You pretend to look calm, so does the wolf,—
yet it dies. I do not believe you,—and now I see
you tremble."

· Ali's frame was quivering with the muscular exertion of forcing open the stubborn iron.

"Fear death!" echoed the Arab, with a scornful
smile. "I have seen it too often; let your father's
son tremble; your brother would have killed me and

I took his life. I shrink not from the penalty; take my life and be satisfied."

"He confesses it, and braves me!" muttered Mahmoud through his clenched teeth, and his eyes glared as he dashed the fatal bullet into the barrel and rammed it down on the charge. "Have I lived to be braved by a vile Bedawi! Your life pay for his? No! not the lives of all your tribe; but," continued he, "though you do not fear, have you not left those in your accursed tent, whose pangs will contribute to my vengeance? Ha! have I stung you? you shall think of that for a space, before I take your dog's life."

The heart of Ali sunk within him, as he found himself utterly unable, without betraying his exertions, to force open the iron link; his only hope of escape from death was the probability of Mahmoud's coming within his reach; the remaining chain which held him was four feet long, and this with his own stride, would give him a lunge of eight feet, and as it is usual in these cases of judicial murder to put the muzzle of the gun to the victim's breast, the chance was possible.

Mahmoud, however, having primed his gun, seemed determined not to give him that chance of escape, and free from all apprehension of losing his revenge, pleased himself with cat-like ferocity, in playing with his victim. He went to the far end of the small room, and began taking deliberate aim, first at his victim's head and then at his heart. Ali shifted his position from side to side to deceive him.

"Why don't you shoot?" he said, "you could
not hit a camel at that distance! See how his hand
shakes! his heart would shake more if I was free!
There, finish! is not your brother waiting for his
revenge?"

Mahmoud, who had controlled himself all this
time with the greatest difficulty, could no longer restrain his fury; he rushed upon him to place the
muzzle to his breast with a yell of rage, when Ali, with
one bound, sprang upon his foe, and before he could
recover from his astonishment, had seized the gun,
and felled him to the earth with the iron manacle on
his wrist, completing his work by shooting him
through the head with his own gun:—and he was
free!

Having succeeded thus far, his next care was to
secure his retreat; first disengaging himself from the
chains, he fastened the door within, and then hastily
changed his own upper dress for that of his senseless
enemy, the soldier's high yellow boots concealed the
shackles on his legs, while the manacles on his wrists
were covered by the folds of his hayk; he gave a
paler tinge to his bronzed face, with the white wash
dust from the walls, he then attired Mahmoud in his
coarse hayk, and taking the precaution of reloading
the gun, he walked quietly out, with the hood of the
burnoose muffling his face, the keeper only making a
passing remark reflecting on his tardiness. As he
expected, he found Mahmoud's horse at the gate, this
he mounted, and pursued his way at a slow pace, but

striking into the less frequented streets, until he entered a long arched passage; here he dismounted, looped the bridle to the high pommel, and fixing a small thorny branch under the girth to act as spurs, he let him loose, and the horse bounded down the street kicking and plunging, and disappeared round the corner; ne thus cut off the clue to his discovery, should he be pursued, and then made his way to where his own horse awaited him.

CHAPTER XI.

HE Chief of the Woled abu Sebah had long been meditating an inroad into the Sultan's territory, and this, the arrival of Yusuf had caused him to accelerate. After despatching Ali, he gave orders to strike the tents, and be ready for marching before dawn, consequently, instead of the stillness which usually prevailed during the night, all was bustle and confusion in preparation for departure, large fires blazed in all directions, round which flitted the dark forms of the Arabs, arranging their arms and accoutrements, packing tents, saddling horses; while the din of hammers, the screaming of camels, and neighing of horses, mingled with the voice of a multitude, and the surging swell of thousands in motion.

Before sunrise every tent was struck, and everything loaded for the march; the whole company now separated into two bands, the larger, consisting of the women, and children, and aged, on camels, and the flocks, with a sufficient number of men for their protection; these took their course southward further into the Desert. The other band of about five thousand horsemen, armed with double guns across their pommels, besides swords and dirks, were to march northward taking Terudant in their route. Each man carried a small supply of provisions, consisting of dates and barley-meal. Several hundred camels accompanied them, carrying spare ammunition and provisions, but though starting so lightly equipped they had every intention of returning more heavily laden with the spoils of their more industrious but less warlike neighbours. As the first troop was diminishing from view, the chief commanded his standard to be unfurled, and mounted his charger: an attendant handed him a bowl of milk, which he first tasted, and then poured over his horse's mane, a ceremony to invoke protection during the journey. He galloped down the front of his line of men, or rather the semicircle which they formed, with a word of salute or kindness to all that came within his ken, he then stopped in their front, and thus addressed them, in a clear, sonorous voice: "Praise be to the one God! Brothers, what shall I say? Will ye be slaves of the Sultan, or will ye stand by the banner of Hamet Ibn Ishem?"

A loud shout of "Long live our chief!" drowned for an instant his voice, and all again was silent.

"It is well, brothers! Ye are true sons of Ishmael, and when the battle comes, let every Arab stand by his brother. What! shall the lord of the Sahel pay tribute to the son of the town? Shall the warrior bow to the plough-driver? Henceforth shall every man live free in his tent, without fear of having the bread taken from

his children, to raise taxes for a stranger. Does the
Sultan want tribute, let him come and seek it; but
instead of gold, he will find lead and steel, and the
bones of his troops shall whiten the red sands of the
Sahara. We now go north, to repay ourselves for what
we have already lost. The provinces are rich, and we
will reap a hundredfold for what has been taken from
us. But one word of warning: let no innocent blood
bring a curse on our tents. I command and entreat ye
to respect women and children, and not to hurt the
unresisting; let mercy follow submission, then shall
success attend our arms, a blessing attend our steps,
and we shall return to our tents in peace. Brothers,
shall we pray?"

All then with raised hands joined in the Fetha, or
prayer of praise and adoration, after which they commenced their march to the province of Suse; and when
far away, they looked back on the scene of their late
camp, there was nothing visible but a broad dark spot,
over which the vultures were hovering.

Various surmises were passing among the Arabs,
with respect to the object of Yusuf's coming, and
having concluded that he had brought intelligence
favourable to this expedition, they were well disposed
towards him, independently of his being the guest of
their chief. As soon as the Sheik could find time, he
rode up to Yusuf, who was mounted on an ambling
mule, plodding along in a rather desponding state of
mind, lest he should return too late, and find Azora's
fate beyond their help.

"Cheer up, O friend," said the Sheik, "we have sent Sheik Ali on in haste to Marocco; he is to be trusted, fear not. I have now much to attend to, but I have appointed you a companion and protector on the road; Sheik Ayoub Er Rami is a good man, he is, as God made him, a good warrior and honest, but fond of hearing himself talk; will it not amuse you by the way? He has been in the towns, and is accustomed to strangers, some of these Arabs of mine never saw a house, and when they do, they only wonder why you should build houses of stone that will last longer than you can use them. Sheik Ayoub!" he called out, and Ayoub, who had been discussing with his friends the probable plunder they would reap, dashed forward to the side of the chief, bringing his horse on his haunches, and ploughing up the sand with his hind hoofs.

"You have a good seat and a good horse," said the chief smiling, as he shook the dust from his burnoose. "This, our guest, is placed in your charge, you will protect him against friend or foe, until I relieve you. Have I not put confidence in you? and is it not well placed?"

Ayoub bowed to his horse's crest. "There is not an Arab who would not risk his life for the guest of our chief: therefore, O Sheik, friends we fear not: and may the Prophet put him in danger of an enemy, that I may prove myself worthy of your trust."

"Avert the omen!" said the Sheik, "I shall be satisfied without such proof. May your prayer not be granted!"

Ayoub was a small, neat figure, with a pair of formidable moustaches, a pointed beard, but no whiskers; he had formerly lived in Marocco, taking service under the Sultan, there he had been obliged to adopt the caftan and turban, but had very soon returned to the independence of the Desert; this, however, had given him more neatness in his dress, and an affectation of knowledge bordering on conceit. He was a great talker, which was facilitated, as his comrades jokingly assured him, by the absence of several teeth, lost in some fray; he was well knit, though short, and when laughed at for his size, he was always ready with a proverb, as " Iron is sold by the quintal, steel by the ounce." The only peculiarity about him in other respects, was that he carried a brace of small pocket pistols in his belt, this joined to his being a good rifle-shot, had acquired him the surname " Er Rami, the Marksman."

" My name," said he in answer to Yusuf's inquiry, " your lord's name (may peace attend it!) is Ayoub Ibn Aisa Ibn Yarib Sebaie, they choose to call me Er Rami, to laugh at my beard, because I carry these children of the gun; but when they have seen them bite, young as they are, they do not laugh at them in the hand of an enemy. Then they open the mouth of astonishment. A Christian gave them to me, may the Prophet enlighten him before his death! They are good men, the Christians, men of trust, they would not break their word to save a ship. The Moors are not worthy to be their grooms; but give me your ear," said he, leaning

from his saddle towards Yusuf, apparently to whisper
his secret, when he shouted out, "they eat pig !"

"Oh, abominable!" exclaimed the equally scandal-
ized Jew; and all the Christians' merits were wrecked
on the reef of prejudice.

Yusuf, however, nothing loth to relieve the mono-
tony of the journey, by encouraging the loquaciousness
of his companion, asked him where he had met with
Christians, and if he had been to Suerah.

Ayoub, only too glad to find a listener, brightened
up as he slung his long bridle round his neck, and let
his horse follow his own pace, that his hands might be
free to accompany his tongue. "Gently, child," this
was to his horse, who knew as well as his master, that
he had work before him, and had no intention of fretting.
"Inshallah, I have seen things, as you say. El Suerah !
Yes, I have seen El Suerah. The Nazarenes call it
Mogadore, after the sanctuary of the Saint Sidi Mog-
dul (his peace be on us !). Well, before I went to the
merchant's house, I said to my head, 'If Ayoub does
not dress himself like a Kaid, or a Taleb, the infidel
will despise him, and I shall appear small in their eyes:'
so I put on a turban of white muslin, as big as that,"
holding his hands a foot and a half from each side of
his head, "then I put on a green caftan and a hayk,
perfumed with sandal-wood, and followed by a boy
with a present of dates and oranges, I went to the
merchant's house. As I was going to enter, out comes
a black soldier, who was sitting in the gate.

"'Where are you going in peace?' said he, he did

not see whom he was speaking to, for his eyes were one half closed with fat, and the other half with importance.

"'Going,' said I, 'to see the merchant,' and I advanced.

"'Tell me who you are,' said he, 'and I will inquire if you can be admitted.'

"This set me laughing. 'Did I come to see the Sultan?' said I; 'when I do, I don't expect to find such a gate-keeper, so take your head from whence you brought it, and find a place to pray in.' And I pushed him out of my path. But my slipper-counter barred the doorway again.

"'You are not in the woods,' says he, quite furious, 'people's houses are not to be entered by force here, as you will find when you eat the stick, for all your turban is as big as a Cuscusoo dish.'

"I was beginning to lose patience. 'I tell you what, O dog of evil race, if we were in the woods, you would defile your beard in the dust, when you presumed to approach my presence; as it is, if you don't save your breath, and stop your tongue from wagging, I shall be compelled to shorten it an inch.' And I was thinking seriously of doing so, when the merchant, attracted by the dispute, looked over the upper gallery to know what was the matter. 'Is this the way, O merchant,' said I, 'that you treat your guests? Behold I come to seek the shadow of your tents, when this evil-eyed slipper-hunter, who calls himself a Moslem, presumes to stop me at the gate; and if it is by your orders, it is no credit to your hospitality.' The merchant looked at me with a peculiar smile.

"'Welcome, O my friend!' said he, in the tongue of the Arab. 'I always tell this slave of the Sultan, to distinguish people; he knows not the difference between a cat and a lion; you must forgive him.'

" I said to myself, 'If the Moslem is a fool, the Christian is wise, and can see through a turban.' Then the merchant took me into a beautiful room, with windows of glass, and tables of precious wood covered with china and crystal; and round the walls were mirrors, and pictures of houris, and everything fit for a Sultan; and I said to myself, 'O Ayoub! hast thou not found the palace of Alla-ed-Din?' After I had looked about a little, the merchant told me to sit, and brought me a small table, with a back made of cane, and a bar for the feet; with such a turban on, what could I do? I sat down on it, and found it was a just fit, neither too small, nor too large, and I was afraid to move for fear of falling, so I put my hands down under my hayk, and held on by the sides of the chair. I began to think I was a ' father of the ears,' passing myself for what I was not, and I doubted but the infidel thought so too; but I forgive him for laughing at my beard, for the lesson he taught me, as I had told him I was one of the palace guards from Marocco.

" While I was thus perched, like a water-melon on a plate, the merchant brought out a handsome gun, inlaid with silver and ivory, and gave it me to look

K

at. My Arab blood could never resist a horse or a gun; off my guard, I stretched out my hand to take it, lost my balance, and down I came. The merchant sprang forward and saved my fall.

"'You have more cushions than chairs in the palace,' said he, 'but sit down on the carpet, and here are cushions.'

"I took his advice and sat down, praying that the inventor of such seats might be condemned to sit on one on the top of the highest mosque in the town, until I took him down. Well, presently came in another young infidel, with blue eyes, and the two began chirruping away like squirrels, then they gave me tea flavoured with ambergris, cakes, and hallowa. When I had eaten God's blessings until I was ashamed, they brought me a little black box; and when I had it in my hand, one of them touched a nail, and (may I be protected!) it began to speak, when I threw it on the carpet, and jumping up, shook my clothes, and invoked curses on Satan, while the two unbelievers were rolling with laughter. I was about to escape, when they got up and begged me to stop, telling me it was only done by art, and not by magic. Then they made it begin again, and lo! as I listened, it warbled beautiful music, a hundred times more sweet than the song of the Oom el hassn or Zurzur. I sat with my hands upraised and my mouth open, exclaiming 'Adjaïb! Wonderful! Wonderful! God is great!' Then it stopped, and behold, I was still in this world! 'O merchant! God increase your blessings,' said I; 'there is only one thing you Christians cannot do, for you can do everything else.'

"'What is that?' said he.

"'O merchant, you cannot prevent death!'

"'We do not wish it, O Sheik; if we do not die, we do not go to heaven.'

"This made me stare: the infidel to go to Ginnah! with the true believer?

"'Would it not be better,' said I, 'to enjoy God's blessings in this world as long as we can, in case of missing the road to the other?'

"'God is merciful,' said he; so not wishing to hurt his feelings, I thought of the pig, and said nothing."

Yusuf, however, thought it as well to put in a word for infidels in general. "Yes," said he, "O Sheik! God is merciful, and is it not written in the gloss of the great Saint Abd el Kader Jilelly, 'Behold three sit at the gate of Paradise, Sidna (our lord) Mohammed, Sidna Moosa, and Sidna Aisa, and when one cometh and it is asked of him, 'What art thou?' he answereth, 'I am a Moslem,' and behold Sidna Mohammed openeth the gate and saith, 'Enter.' And another cometh and saith, 'I am a Jew,' and Sidna Moosa openeth the gate and saith, 'Enter.' And another cometh and saith, 'I am a Christian,' and Sidna Aisa openeth the gate and saith, 'Enter.' And a fourth ,cometh and saith, 'I am a Renegade, I have changed my faith,' so no one openeth unto him, he is accursed!"

"Did our lord, Abd el Kader write that?" said

Ayoub, "wonderful is the mercy of God; but no doubt, in his days, Christians did not eat pig. But where was I? I remember. Well, then, the young infidel with blue eyes took me by the sleeve, and said, ' Come with me, and I will show you *such* a horse as you have not seen in the Sultan's stud;' what could I do? I followed him with alacrity, so we went down into the courtyard, and oh, what a horse! I would walk three days' journey on foot to see such another; his coat was mottled like the ripple of the stream, his neck like a rainbow, his mane, like a curtain of silk, reached to his knees, eyes and legs like the antelope, and broad breasted like a houri; what can I say? I sat down by the wall and blessed him. He was as quiet as a lamb, but when the Christian mounted him he became like a lion, his eye saw everything, his ear heard everything, his hoof disdained everything, and as he paced along, I could have thrown myself under his feet, and let him walk over me.

" ' You are a judge of horses,' said the merchant, ' what do you think of him?'

" ' May evil eyes be averted from him,' said I, ' he is perfect.'

" And when I got on the subject (although not given to talking) I ran on about shoulders and pasterns, fetlocks and hoofs, manes and tails, eyes, nostrils, and genealogies, enough to fill a book, till the merchant was astonished, and must have thought I was a delal.

" ' You have seen horses, O Sheik!' said he,

'but you have not learnt that it is safer to ride a horse that kicks than one you don't know.'

"I saw I was fairly found out, and was obliged to give up the game.

"'I have learnt, O merchant!' said I, 'that the eagle cannot fly with the wings of the ostrich; and if I had not been fool enough to curl my moustachios in a Kaïd's skin, I should not have deserved to have the beard of my father's son laughed at; Sheik Ayoub Sebaïe is not ashamed of his tribe, but in truth these Moors always measure a man by the size of his turban, and I thought you would do the same. Allaw Ackbar! what can I say more?'

"'Although I am a merchant,' said he, 'I don't measure a man with a cloth cubit; come to-morrow in your own dress and I'll show you more, that you have not seen. It is a little at a time, that the sheep gets into the stew-pan.'

"I found that out in time, and by degrees I got accustomed to that dress, and a dozen others, so that none could tell that I had not been born in them.

"I'll tell you another time how I escaped from the town of Teradant with the Kaïd's horse. But to go back to the merchant, I went the next day dressed as I am now.

"'God be praised, Sheik Ayoub!' said he, 'now you are a true son of the Desert, we shall be better friends.' (The slipper-counter did not stop me this time.)

He brought me to a sofa, and we ate and drank, and

praised God; and were as if we had been brought up in the same tent."

"And the pig! you did not eat that?" said Yusuf, laughing.

"God forbid!" said Ayoub, spitting on the ground. " I took an oath of him before eating that there was none in the food; besides he had a Moslem for a cook, and you know he would not touch it. Afterwards, he took me on board his ship, and showed me wonderful things, clocks, and watches, and guns without flints that never missed; matches to light without fire, pictures and astrolabes, and all sorts of wonderful things, till I got giddy with the motion of the ship, and we landed in a boat; I used to go to his house every day, and when I had sold my ostrich-feathers and gum from Soudan, and my camels were rested, and I was about to depart, I thought he would have shed tears; he gave me presents of gunpowder, and a cloth dress of blue, and fine tea, and this pair of pistols; and then he rode on the way with me, two hours' journey. Then he said, ' God be with thee, oh, my brother! and bring thee to thy tents in peace. And now, I beseech thee, if peradventure any of my countrymen should be shipwrecked on the Desert, or fall into the hands of thy people, that thou wilt be kind to them, and befriend them for my sake.' I promised by the bread and salt that was between us, and we parted, and both went on our way sorrowful. How often I remember him, and pray that his house may be prosperous, and that he may be enlightened!"

Here Ayoub rested his chin in his hand in a fit of abstraction, and to recover his breath.

"Poor fellow!" he muttered, "yes, God is great. The English are good, the English are to be trusted; are they not sons of Sultans, oh, why do they eat pig? But now I remember, my friend, the merchant told me he never ate pig, and his cook a Moslem, I don't believe he ever did eat pig, Al hamdo l'Illah, I am sure the friend of Sheik Ayoub never ate pig! Alla Illah!"

"Now tell me," said Yusuf, "where we halt to-night, for we appear to be going the road I came?"

"True," said Ayoub, "we stop at the wells where the Cafila was plundered. That was a clever foray of Ali el Bezz, he brought in a fine booty without any loss; I wish he were with us, for, excepting Sidi Hamed, there is not a better head, or a surer hand on an expedition, between this and El Yemen."

The sun was casting its level rays against the Eastern sky when they reached the rocks, the scene of the late attack. Here they all bivouacked under the spangled canopy; there were two or three tents for the chief and some of the sheiks; of these one was allotted to Yusuf and his escort. After the horses were watered and picketed, Ayoub was sent for to the chief's tent, and returned with an Arab, carrying jars of milk, butter, dates, barley-cakes, and dried ostrich flesh, in strips.

"The chief sends you this poor supper," said Ayoub; "I told him flesh was not lawful for you if you did not kill it; so here are two fowls, you kill them according to your custom, and they are lawful to us; my uncle's son here will cook them; we mount with the moon's rising."

The night was calm, and the fires were beginning to blaze around as the Arabs collected in groups to cook their evening meal. Beyond the hum of a multitude there was very little noise, and as Yusuf and his host sat by their fire, in front of their tent, Yusuf reminded him of his promise to recount his adventures in Teradant.

"Oh, Sheik!" he said, "your adventures are like the Thousand and One Nights, when a man has heard one, lo, he asks for another."

"Bismillah!" said Ayoub, nothing loth to recount his exploits. "As you say I have seen things; let me recollect, it was when I was employed with the men of my tribe plundering the caravans and traders that frequented the market of Teradant with produce and merchandise; for all who did not pay us toll were not spared; have we not a right to custom from goods passing our territories as well as the Sultan? and those who did not pay for protection made no profit by their ventures. So, you see, I had friends in the town who protected me for a share of the booty, and who would not have been long on God's earth had they dared to betray us; thus, O friend, I was in the habit of entering the town in disguise to obtain intelligence of the movements of the merchants. One of our friends kept a kebab-shop, where the sons of the town

collected of an evening to eat kebabs, and drink sher-
bet, and hear the news; he made his force-meat of
sheep's heads, and these when clean boiled were piled
up at the end of the room. I have seen there several
thousands; we formed a recess behind these with
boards, communicating with the back room by a
small door; and here have I often been cooped up
watching the guests, and hearing all their plans and
the value of their goods when they little thought the
sheep's skulls had eyes in them. Another was a grain-
merchant, and there I have been buried in barley up to
my neck, with a fanega measure with a hole in it
over my head, and heard who was going with money
to the douars to buy grain. And, behold, were they
not astonished when Sheik Ayoub met them on the
Sahel with the salutation of peace, and asked one for
the twenty pieces of gold that were in his camel's
saddle, and another for the three hundred ducats sewn
up in the right sleeve of his djilabea?

"One day riding with some of my band, a few
miles from the town, I met a horseman in a fine hayk,
and green velvet coat.

"'Peace to you, O Abdallah,' said I, 'where is my
lord going?'

"'To you, peace,' said he; 'I go to the douar to
buy a sheep.'

"'Has my lord a pass from Sheik Ayoub?'
said I.

"'Am I a trader to need a pass?' said he; 'I am a
poor man.'

"'God is merciful, O Sheik!' said I; 'as you are a poor man I will only take your nose-bag.'

"'The nose-bag of my horse!' said he, turning pale; 'know you. not that it is unlucky to part with that? I will redeem it; behold three dirhems, the price of the sheep, take them.'

"'No,' said I; 'I must have the nose-bag.'

"'I will give you the hayk,' said he, 'or my caftan of cloth, for I fear ill-luck to my horse.'

"'No, by Allah!' said I; 'I will not plunder a poor man, nothing but the nose-bag: have I not sworn?' and I hooked it from his pommel with the end of my gun. 'And now, Sheik Abdallah,' said I, 'follow me, your nose-bag shall be restored, and no harm shall befall your horse.' Then his face brightened, and he followed me joyfully. When we came to a place among the trees where there was a surface of smooth sand, I dismounted my men, and the horses being all tied up, I traced a circle on the sand, and made the men all sit around, and thus I addressed the unfortunate one :—

"'You wonder, perhaps, why I would only take from you your nose-bag—but know, O Sheik Abdallah, that I am a man of a charitable disposition, but possessed of no property except a ring, which once belonged to Allah ed Deen; and as I was desirous of repairing the sanctuary of our patron saint, and building a fountain for wayfarers, I rubbed the ring, when, lo, one of the jinn, the slave of the ring, appeared, and stood before me with his hands crossed on his breast, and his eyes looking on the ground, saying,—

" 'I hear and obey.'

" Then I said, 'I have need of fifty pieces of gold.'

" And he said, 'On the head and eyes;' and he disappeared for the space that a feather might fall to the ground, and came back, saying, 'There is not a piece of gold in the treasure-house of the jinn.'

" And I said, 'Woe unto thee.'

" But he said, 'Let not my lord be wroth, there is a remedy ; let my lord ride in the morning towards Teradant, and there shall meet him a man of a handsome countenance wearing a green caftan, embroidered with gold, and a fillelly hayk, you will take from him nothing but the nose-bag of his horse, and having put therein the ring, you will make a circle on the ground, and lay it in the midst, covering it with a hayk, and peradventure my lord's wishes will be accomplished.'

" My friend of the fine coat looked like the man who is going to the bastinado, whilst I made my preparations. Then I sat down within the circle, and put my hands under the hayk, and when I withdrew my hand, lo, a piece of gold! and again I put in my hand, and lo, another piece of gold! And the eyes of my Arabs were rounded, and their mouths open, and they felt the pieces of gold to see if they were real, and behold, they were bintekas of fine gold, and I ceased not to count until I had counted fifty pieces of gold! Then I arose, and said, 'The jinn has accomplished my desire, and now, O Sheik, I give thee a peçeta of five dirhems for the use of thy nose-bag, take it, and go in peace, lest ill-luck befall thy horse.' And the Moor's face was white, and his features trembled, as though he had seen an Afreet, but my face was as a deep well. Then he mused a little, and said, ' O Sheik ! the slave of the ring is no other than a woman. A woman betrayed our father Adam, on whom be peace; and woman betrayed Suleiman the wise; and who are we that we should escape ? ' so he mounted his horse and departed."

" And was he right in his guess, O Sheik?" said Yusuf.

" He was, and he was not," said Ayoub. "I will tell you how it happened; Sheik Abdallah is a relation of the Kaïd of Teradant, and I had found out that he was about to depart on a trading expedition to purchase gum and ostrich-feathers; and as he was going alone, and taking no goods with him for barter, I knew he must have sent money before, or would carry it with him; he lived not far from the kebab-shop, and the houses of Teradant being all flat-roofed, and the partition walls low, I have frequently walked all over the town at night on the roofs. So one dark night I went to the top of his house, and sat down, overlooking the room where he was, on the opposite side of the court; it was hot, and he was sitting in the gallery outside with his wife. There was a great deal talked that did not concern me; at last his wife said, ' O my lord, when do you go to Tafilelt ? ' and he answered, On such a day. Then she caressed him and said, 'The veils of Tafilelt are as fine muslins of Ind; will not my lord buy one for his slave, that she may appear honourable in the eyes of the women that go to the baths, and they will say, 'Behold, this is the wife of Abdallah the merchant!'

"'O light of my eyes!' said he, 'have I any money to buy fillelly hayks, or fine clothes? I have none.'

"'False!' said she, 'are there not fifty pieces of gold that my lord ordered me to sew into his horse's nose-bag?'

"Then he smote her on the mouth with his slipper, and said, 'Peace, O unlucky! lest some of the slaves hear thee. Is that money mine? is it not to pay for merchandise which I owe?'

"Well, as I had heard all I wanted to know, I left them to make up their quarrel, and that is how the woman was the slave of the ring. Abdallah the Moor, enraged by the loss of his money, complained to the Governor; and a stricter watch than ever was kept to take me, and even a reward of one hundred dirhems was proclaimed by the public crier, to any one who would bring me bound before the Kaïd. Well, I laughed at all this, till one unlucky morning I was going into the town, disguised as a Berebber peasant, driving a donkey laden with firewood; and as other cattle were going in and coming out, there was a crush, and I got enraged, and cursed, forgetting to change my voice; and, behold, when I looked up,

Abdallah the Moor, sitting on his horse, waiting to go forth, and his eyes were fixed on me like two coals in white rings. I had on a tattered cloak, with a hood. I saw that he knew me, though he said nothing, and I passed on, and went to my friend the cook's shop. Whilst I was debating about leaving the town, my friend came to me with evil tidings : 'Knowest thou, Sheik Ayoub,' said he, 'that thou hast been recognised by some one, and search is made everywhere to take thee. The gates of the town are closed, and guards set on the walls to prevent thy escape.'

"'God is great,' said I; 'was a panther or a bird ever kept in a cage without a roof? May the Kaïd's beard be defiled! probably to-morrow, or the day after, they will open the gates.'

"'This time,' said he, 'you are in danger. What had you to do to meddle with the Kaïd or his relations? he is furious and vows vengeance against any one that hides you; but we have eaten bread and salt together.'

"'God be praised!' said I, 'and we have eaten the money of the Sultan's subjects together; and, moreover, is it not known that the man who should betray Sheik Ayoub Sebaïe, he and his family would be made into kebabs, and roasted in the flames of his own house?'

"'May evil eyes be averted!' said he, 'but know further that the Kaïd has taken up his residence in the kiosk over the gate, and none can go out without a pass from him.'

"'Has he so?' said I, as a thought struck me. 'God is merciful! then I will go out by that gate. If it is written, he may repent of bringing the lion to bay.'

"I knew that the Kaïd had a son, a boy of six years old, of whom he was very fond, and from whom he never separated; and if I could find them alone, my escape was secure, and the Kaïd's beard would be defiled.

"I remained hidden that day, and the next, hearing the search that was being made for me; and the next evening, having received intelligence that the people had dispersed from the audience, and that the Governor was alone in the kiosk; about an hour before the evening prayer I sallied out dressed as a Moor of the town, and reached the gate without interruption, but in dread lest some of the soldiers lounging about might recognise me. I sent one of the guards with a message to the Kaïd, to say that I wished to give information regarding Sheik Ayoub, and wanted a private interview. He soon returned, and I followed him to the presence of the Kaïd. The latter was sitting on his mattress and cushions, with his little boy by his side; he had a chess-board and ivory pieces, and was trying to teach the game to the child; he was so pre-occupied that he just looked up when I entered, and made a motion for me to sit, which I did.

"'Father,' said the child, 'what is the use of the Roh?'

"'To protect the Sultan when in danger, my dear boy.'

" ' And so,' said he, without taking his attention from the board, 'you have brought intelligence of Ayoub El Rami; if you can help me catch him, I will change his name to El Eshara' (the mark.)

" ' There!'—here he castled the king—' now the Shah is safe.'

" ' And if the Shah can't move,' suggested the child, while I had uncovered my head, and freed my hands for action.

" I could not help smiling at the security of the two, near one whom the Kaïd might suppose his greatest enemy.

" ' God be praised!' said the Kaïd, delighted at the precociousness of his pet, 'you will soon be a master. If the Shah can't escape, it is Shah Mãt.'

" ' But what have you, friend, to say to me? Where is this Shietan Ayoub to be found?'. Here he looked round, and found my eyes fixed upon him, when it was amusing to see the change that came over his features, and his terror at finding himself in such dangerous company. I was tempted to echo his ' Shah Mãt.'

" ' You require information, O Kaïd,' I said, 're-specting Ayoub Ibn Yarib Sebaïc, and I knew of no one more able to give it than *himself*; he expected a more courteous reception than you lately promised him, but having no desire to be your target, he intends to leave this place unharmed.' Seeing me so quiet, his terror subsided, and he thought to intrap me by cunning.

"'By the beard of the Prophet!' said he, 'I did not believe all these accusations against you; I intend you no evil, I will give orders that you be not molested, you may depart in peace.'

"'Is Sheik Ayoub a father of the ears?' said I; 'he is come to claim the reward, and cannot leave my lord's roof empty-handed.'

"'Who are we,' said the Kaïd, beginning to chafe, 'that your father's son should dare to come and spit on the beard of the Sultan's Kalifa?'

"I had played the fool long enough, and, seeing he was about to summon assistance, I suddenly seized his arm, and placed a pistol to his breast.

"'Mark me,' said I, 'the first call for help sends a ball through your body;' and I swore an irrevocable oath. 'And now listen: I intend to leave this town by the gate, and in safety; and to ensure this, I take your child as a hostage. If I am not molested I will return him in safety, but should I be pursued—' here I whispered in his ear, 'By Allah, he dies! Now you are in my power, and let your head teach you wisdom.'

"The Kaïd, seeing my determination, thought it better to submit; fortunately the child, who was a little frightened at first, was docile; and when his father reluctantly resigned him, unconscious of his danger, he let me take him in my arms, thinking he was only going for a ride, and coming back. I then went to the door and called out, 'Who waits?'

"'Your slave,' answered the guard from below.

L

" 'The Governor commands you to bring his horse caparisoned to the gate, and his gun.—Away! delay not!'

" 'On my head and eyes be it,' said the soldier.

" As the horses were always kept ready saddled, I had not long to wait. I could not help feeling for the old man, notwithstanding his ill-will. When I was about to take away his boy, he would have bound himself by any oath, rather than expose him to this peril, but I dared not trust him. I took him to the balcony overlooking the plain, 'You sought my life,' I said, ' but you are forgiven; and may you behave to me and mine, should we fall into your power, as I behave to this child. Now behold the sanctuary on the top of the nearest hill, when I reach that in peace I will deliver the boy to the Marabt who keeps it; but, should you rashly pursue me, his blood be on your own head, my hands are clean.'

" It is painful to see a man accustomed to command eat the bitter apple of humiliation. I had brought him so low that I could almost have trusted him, when the tears were in his eyes, as he kissed his child, entreating me to be cool, and not influenced by any false alarm or appearance of danger.

" 'Allah! Allah!' he cried in anguish, 'if I lose my child, my power will have cost me dear. May your journey be prosperous!' Then calling the soldier he said, 'Go with my friend to the gate; he is going to the sanctuary to pray for my son; let no man stay him, you have heard.'

"I went down with the child in my arms, and mounting the horse, a noble animal he was, and taking the gun, which was also very valuable, across the pommel, I rode deliberately out of the town, congratulating myself on the success of my stratagem. The saint's tomb was about two miles from the gates, and I considered that quite a sufficient start in case of pursuit. As I rode slowly across the plain, I could see the Governor walking up and down his balcony, and wishing to give him a severe lesson, knowing he was watching my movements, I purposely stopped to speak to every horseman I met on the road. At one time two horsemen came galloping at full speed from the direction of the town,—they were only exercising; but as I turned my horse's head towards them, I could plainly see the old man wringing his hands in painful suspense; and as they came near me, he sat down and hid his face in his hayk, whilst the child was prattling away, and in the highest delight at his excursion. And that is how Sheik Ayoub escaped from the town with the horse of the Kaïd Abdallah Ibn Sadek; and now it is time to sleep, for we start with the dawn."

CHAPTER XII.

AZORA.

HE time allowed to Azora to give 'a definite answer to the Sultan's proposal had quickly passed away. She had not been allowed much time for preparation. for the awful fate that menaced her in case of non-compliance, on account of the intrusive officiousness of the inmates of the hareem, who with childish kindness did all in their power to alleviate her distress, which they attributed to her regret at leaving her relations and friends; never for a moment imagining that she could have courage to relinquish the pleasures of life, and brave death in its most revolting shape, when it might be avoided by what appeared to them so slight a sacrifice; and they already looked upon her as a future companion. Some of the ladies of the hareem had handsome features which the absence of expression rendered valueless. They were the fair faces of women who are born, brought up, and die with scarcely (except in very childhood) any communication with their kind,—whose whole world from birth to death is comprised within three or four rooms with blank walls. This sedentary existence is conducive to the obesity, which to Moorish taste is considered the perfection of female beauty; and the women adopt every means to encourage this natural tendency; one of these is the same as the plan adopted with us for fattening turkeys. A paste composed of new bread and oleaginous seeds, is formed into balls, the size of a pigeon's egg, and a certain number of these are swallowed whole, washed down with water; this is done daily until the required standard of deformity is reached. The inmates of the Sultan's hareem had the advantage of gardens, into which their rooms opened. These gardens were planted with fruit-trees and vines on trellis; and in the centre of the one they now looked on, was a basin and fountain, that threw its spray on high and cooled the air, confined as it was within high walls. One of the ladies was about Azora's own age, and had become very much attached to her, she had claims to beauty of face and form, which the fattening process, at her age, had not yet destroyed. Her black hair was ornamented with pearls and beads of fine gold; her flashing eye was brightened by the kohal, with which her lids were tinged; a latent smile played round a mouth which should have been lovely; she was a creature of mere life .with no thought but for such trivial happiness as she might snatch in her contracted sphere on earth, and for anything beyond, probably never thought of it at all! She wore an embroidered green velvet jacket, fitted to the form, and flowing muslin trousers, over this dress was wound a fine hayk. Her name was Oom-el-Zin. While some of them were swallowing balls, and others staining their feet and

hands in patterns with henna, or employed in other
ways, Azora and her friend wandered out, following
one of the grape-walks, till they came to a secluded
bower formed by the foliage, and furnished with carpets
and cushions. Here they sat down.

"This day will seal my fate, O my sister!" said
Azora, mournfully. Her friend said nothing in reply,
but her habitual smile forsook her now sorrowful face,
and tears stood in her eyes.

"Why are you so kind to me?" Azora continued,
embracing her. "To part from you will more embitter
the cup that I must drink."

"Oh, say not you will leave me," said Oom-el-Zin,
throwing her arms around Azora, "you make me
shudder when you talk of death, and yet I begin to
believe you are in earnest. But no! you can not—you
dare not—die!"

"The God of Israel will support me in death," said
Azora, solemnly. "A few short years, and who, of all
those who now behold my doom, will be alive to tell
how died the Hebrew girl?—and shall I barter an
eternity, compared to which centuries are but as those
glittering drops of water to the firmament they mock,
for power to drag out my few remaining years in guilt
and infamy? What can I not dare for the love of
God, to whom I owe all? and when His hand is heavy
upon me, shall I not say, with the Arabian patriarch—
'The Lord hath given—the Lord hath taken—blessed'
be the Lord.'"

"Talk not so, O dear, dear Azora! I would rather

live out my life in a prison, without the light of day, only I would not die. Oh, we will be so happy here together! Oh, you cannot sacrifice yourself—you, so young, so beautiful; you make me so miserable. Oh, live! and stay with us." But in vain the tearful eye of the affectionate girl looked for a kindred feeling in the face of the enthusiastic Jewess.

"Alas! for you, my dear girl," she said; "did you possess the hope of a glorious future, you would not dread that which must, sooner or later, come to all.—But lo! we are called. The hour is come."

They arose to return, as one of the women attendants had come to summon Azora to the Sultan's presence.

"I almost distrust my own weak heart," she continued; "but the Lord of Hosts is my strength, the God of Israel is my refuge."

Tenderly embracing her weeping and disconsolate companion, she accompanied the messenger, and was conducted to the same apartment that had been the scene of her previous trial.

The short period that had intervened—but which to her had been an age of mental suffering—showed its influence on her frame; her pale cheeks witnessed to the anguish that had preyed on her soul; but now they flushed with a hectic glow, from the strong temporary excitement of her position, and her beauty was not the less transcendant.

The Sultan was reclining on the cushions when she entered, but rose to meet her.

"Welcome, O beautiful one!" said he; "how long

to me has been the time, deprived of your presence! If it has changed your resolution, I am content. Come you now to enjoy with me life, happiness, and triumph, or ——" His brow darkened as she stood silent and motionless, and he could perceive no signs of acquiescence.   There was a pause.

"Finish, O my lord!" said Azora, at length, "'or death,' you would say,—God's will be done!—Yet, O my lord!" and she threw herself at his feet, "pause ere you pronounce my doom. Oh, throw not away the high privilege of mercy. If in truth you loved me, could your tongue consign me to death? Impossible! To torture? Oh, the thought is horrible! Save me! O king, save me! though not for my sake, for your own, for the sake of your undying fame. Oh, will you for a caprice forego the satisfaction of doing a noble deed, and tarnish with blood the annals of a beneficent reign? What will be said among the nations when it is known that the Sultan Mulai Abderrahman has shed the innocent blood of a woman? Oh, be merciful, and spare me!"

The Sultan was moved by this appeal, seconded by her imploring action and anguished face, but was too intent on his purpose to give way to more than a passing emotion.

"Arise," he said, "why kneel to me; are you not the arbitress of your own fate? 'Tis I that implore you to save yourself and have pity on me. That I wish not your death, which is forfeit to the law, witness my patience, and the efforts I have made to change your mad resolve. But that I love you, rather would I see you die, than given to the arms of another. What! shall I see a vile slave possess that which his sovereign sued for in vain? But what is this strange infatuation? Oh, change but your faith, and I will raise you from your base state, exposed to insult and persecution, to be the favourite of a Sultan, with slaves to obey your every wish—power to protect your friends—in short, all, all that a king can offer, shall be yours! Why will you thus madly persist in throwing away your life? Speak but the word——"

"All this, O my lord," said Azora, firmly, "shall not bribe me to betray my God; I ask mercy, but I ask it unconditionally. What law have I broken? what crime have I committed, for which to sue for pardon? yet the mercy you offer is more cruel than your unjust sentence of death! Were you a just king, my false accusers—for you know them false— would ere this have paid the penalty of their perjury. I am in your power, and may God help me! I will endure all you can inflict rather than save my innocent life by a dishonourable and criminal compromise. But oh, how shall this black deed sully the brightness of your reign to all posterity! We shall meet again before the tribunal of the Lord of kings, and before whom Sultans will tremble."

She had drawn herself up to her full height while thus speaking, and her bosom heaving, and her eyes flashing with enthusiasm, she stood like an inspired prophetess, but with a martyr's calm resolve. The

Sultan had thus far endeavoured to stifle his feelings, but now his rage became ungovernable.

"It is thus, then, that you defy me," he said: "now hear the alternative. If the thought is dreadful, how will you bear the reality? How will you bear to be the gaze and scoff of a ruffian rabble—to be stripped by the rude hands of the executioner? How will your delicate frame bear the agony when thrown alive into the burning pile? Then, when the hot fire slowly seizes on each writhing limb, and every scorched nerve overwhelms your soul with agonising torments, then—when too late, you will repent your refusal of my proffered mercy. Then—when too late, you will wish to recall this lost opportunity, and your tender limbs will fall a lifeless corse among the smouldering ashes. This is your doom! I have said!"

With his face and frame agitated by his passion, and casting a malignant look on the lovely but trembling girl, he rushed from the apartment. Azora's heart sickened within her, as she listened, with suspended breath, to the description of the torture that awaited her. It was a fearful trial, and she had wellnigh sunk under it. Finding herself alone, her firmness forsook her; she threw herself on the cushions, and burst into an agony of tears, and convulsive sobs shook her frame; but this was a luxury, compared to the horrible feeling that came over her, when, after a time, she raised her deadly pale face, from which all traces of tears had passed away, and remained with her eyes fixed on vacancy, while an icy chill seemed to

curdle her heart's blood, and a tightness in the throat
oppressed her almost to suffocation, as she realized the
appalling picture of an ignominious death thus presented to her as the alternative of her resistance. Was
it surprising that, at such a trying moment, her existence suspended trembling on the verge of the tomb,
and failing nature standing terror-struck on the brink
of the awful abyss that separated her from eternity,—
she, so young, should shrink from taking the fatal
plunge. Already was she beginning to parley with
conscience,—already was her resolution wavering, and
the bright crown of martyrdom, which seemed on the
point of encircling her brow, was ascending from whence
it was offered, as the love of life, and the enjoyments
of the world, were resuming their dominion over her
young heart, when, suddenly, overcoming herself with
an almost supernatural effort, she fell on her knees,
and poured out her anguished soul before God, imploring Him to take the love of the world from her
heart, and strengthen her to support the trials that
awaited her for her attachment to her faith. The
struggle was past, her prayer was heard. She arose
from her knees, a radiant smile lighting up her angel
face, and she could now calmly contemplate death, as
a passage from her sufferings here to everlasting life in
the presence of her Redeemer.

A stranger, unacquainted with the peculiar character and customs of this people, might naturally be disposed to ask, why the Sultan should be so scrupulous
in his conduct towards a Jewess, of a race, moreover,

described to be in a state of semi-servitude. It was exactly in the fact of her being a Jewess, that the obstacles the Sultan had to contend with lay.

If it had been possible that a Moorish woman could have made an objection to becoming a Sultana, the same compulsion would have been used, as is used in two-thirds of the marriages among them, in which the parties have no previous knowledge of each other. Moorish women are only too ready to become inmates of the Sultan's harem. But in the case of a Jewess, of a despised religion, the Sultan dare not avow his real object. To have taken Azora, as a Jewess, would have raised a fanatical insurrection. There is, moreover, among the higher classes of the Moors, much of that chivalric spirit which distinguished them in Spain, if, indeed, it is not of Arabian origin, and which invested woman with a sacred character,—indeed the very word harem implies sanctity. Again, it is the policy of the Sultan to encourage the Jews, who alone of his subjects engage in foreign commerce, from which he derives the greater part of his revenue, and his only hold on them consists in the protection afforded to their religion. Interfere with their observances deliberately, and he is apprehensive of their abandoning these pursuits, and endeavouring to remove their wealth from the country. So long as Azora asserted her Jewish faith, he might take her life, but she was in no danger of any other indignity; and it is probably owing to the unswerving attachment of the Jews to their faith, even to martyrdom, and its consequent want of success, that this false

accusation is so rarely resorted to. The enraged despot,
incapable of admiring the heroic fortitude of his helpless captive, was incensed beyond measure by the
failure of all his attempts to intimidate, or persuade her
into compliance. Vacillating between his passion and
his fears, he was tempted to violate the commands of the
Koran, which forbids a Moslem to marry an infidel;
deterred, on the other hand, by the danger of the experiment, especially at the present juncture, when the
principal Arab chiefs were in rebellion, and it behoved
him to secure the fidelity of his troops, whose attachment might be entirely alienated by any sacrilegious
breach of the laws of religion. As a last resource, he
determined to put in execution a plan he had often
thought of in his moments of rage and disappointment.
He resolved to expose her to the wild beasts, of which
there were several in his menagerie; he doubted not
that her terror would then overcome what he considered
her obstinacy, and should this fail, her death was
decreed. Among the wild beasts was a magnificent
lion, this animal was comparatively tame, being kept
well fed, and under his keeper's control. Trusting to
his docility, the keeper had ventured to lead him about
the town by a rope, he had on one occasion destroyed
a child, and on another struck down and killed an unfortunate donkey with one blow of his enormous paw,
by way of practice, and to show what he could do. It
was to this enormous brute, that the lovely and fragile
girl was to be exposed, and the Sultan could hardly
believe that she would not at once embrace the Koran,

to escape the horrible fate of being torn to pieces.
Moody and slow he took his way to the M'Shouar, and
ordered the keeper to attend and receive his commands.
Here he found the principal Wezeer, Talb Jelool, who,
after the usual obeisance, informed him that he had
matters of importance to communicate. The Sultan
took his seat, and gave his acquiescence with an em-
phatic "Bism' Illah." And the Wezeer producing his
papers, sat at the foot of the carpet, and, waving his
hand to the attendants, they immediately withdrew.

"May my lord's throne be exalted!" he said. "I
have heard that the Arabs are marching northward;
they have already passed through Suse and Draha, and
menace the province of Rahamna; and behold here is
a letter from the Kaïd of Teradant, which I will read
to my lord the Sultan.

"'Praise be to the one God. To the great and
mighty lord, the Khalifa of the Prophet, &c., &c.,
Mulai Abd Er Rahman, from his slave Abd Allah Ibn
Sadek, governor of Teradant. Be it known to my lord,
that his rebel slave, Hamed Ibn Ishem, at the head of
the tribes of Abu Sebah, Tuwat, Al Harib, and others,
amounting to about ten thousand Arabs, have entered
and overrun the province of Suse, carrying off flocks
and camels, and levying tribute in the realm of our
sovereign lord. Having only fifty horsemen, besides
the militia of the town, my lord's servant was unable
to take the field, against such large forces, and would
humbly urge the necessity of sending a body of the
black troops to stop their further depredations, and

protect this town, the walls of which are not strong enough to keep the enemy out, should they attack it. Peace! This 10th day of Saffer, 1248.'"

The Sultan could hardly keep patience during the perusal of this letter. "And has the slave dared," said he, "to attack our territories, as well as refuse us tribute? By the holy Prophet's tomb, the death of every dog of his tribe would ill atone for such an insult. Summon the Berebber tribes of the mountains. Send troops to the assistance of the Kaïd of Teradant! And as soon as we are in a position to take the field, we will scatter their hordes, and drive the remnants to their barren sands."

A soldier here entered, and prostrating himself, rose for permission to speak, and then said, "May it please my lord, the keeper of the wild beasts is in attendance."

"Let him appear," said the Sultan.

And he was immediately dragged in by two soldiers, who threw him violently on his face, and then allowing him to rise to his knees, left him to receive his orders. The keeper of the wild beasts was a Jew, for the Moors say, although they do not believe it, that a lion is of too noble a nature to injure a Jew. He was a brutal-looking fellow, with a cast in his eye,—this had procured him the name of Ain ed Djin, or "Demon eye;" he, was short and square, with a stunted grey beard, he wore the black cap, but had put on a white cloak, and had also fortified himself with copious libations of brandy to appear before the Sultan.

"Have you obeyed my orders, dog?" demanded the Sultan.

"May my lord live for ever!" said Demon-eye, "the lion has been without food nearly four-and-twenty hours, which (may my lord be preserved!) is a long fast, seeing he was accustomed to two sheep daily. If my lord (may he be exalted!) had seen him the other day knock down the donkey, and suck its blood, and afterwards crunch its bones, with as much ease as my lord (exalted of God) would a roasted quail." He had got thus far, with a grin of delight and intoxication on his inhuman countenance.

"Peace, infidel dog!" thundered the Sultan, "lest you forthwith share the same fate. Have we nought better to occupy us but to listen to thy misbegotten speech? I would fain try the truth of the proverb on thy vile carcase, and see whether a lion will eat a Jew. Keep the lion fasting, and have him taken to-morrow to the old Serai, inside the south wall."

"My lord shall be obeyed," said Ain ed Djin, in whom the first part of the Sultan's speech had caused a shudder, regaining his assurance, he continued, "When he has fasted forty-eight hours, he will give my lord (whose throne be exalted) satisfaction, and a fat infidel will be to him as a pistachio nut."

"Slave! Son of a cursed race," exclaimed the Sultan, "what dog's son art thou, that darest to pollute our ears with thy drunken words? Ho! the guards!" and making a sign to them as they entered, Demon-eye was seized and dragged out, perfectly sobered, and was soon taught by a severe and well-merited bastinado, administered with the leather thongs the soldiers wear for the purpose, to be more chary of his words in future; and when he arose writhing from his stripes, he was glad to make his escape and execute his orders.

CHAPTER XIII.

THE FALCON'S SWOOP.

T is very painful to record the fearful trials of this innocent and helpless girl, but truth demands it; and I indulge a hope, that, by drawing attention to the facts, I may enlist the sympathy of those who may have the power, and will exert their influence, for the amelioration of the condition of an unprotected race, and perhaps avert future similar outrages on our common humanity.

This new project of the Sultan soon became known through the town, and affected, with surprise and consternation, the friends who were working for Azora's deliverance. Ali had already some five-and-twenty of his followers in the town; these had introduced themselves as country Arabs with wood, vegetables, or fruit, for sale, while their horses were led by others personating horse-dealers. It is true that all strangers on entering the town were obliged to leave their guns at the gate with the guard till their exit; but this they evaded by carrying a second Moorish gun, while their own shorter pieces were smuggled in, in the loads or otherwise. Ali, however, did not feel himself strong enough for a *coup-de-main*, and was waiting anxiously for the chief, who, while his main body were plundering the provinces, was on his way with a chosen band, with the intention of carrying a foray to the very gates of Marocco, as well to intimidate his enemies as to aid at the same time, whether by stratagem or open force, in the redemption of his Pledge.

Ain ed Djin, a Jew himself, had informed Rachel and Ali, who had met him by appointment, of his orders, but could do nothing to help them. I will draw a veil over the sufferings of Azora's afflicted mother. Ali el Bezz was almost at his wits' end, not but that he would have destroyed every wild beast in the town rather than fail in his trust, but caution was absolutely necessary.

"Could you not poison this lion, O Jew?" said he.

"Doubtless, O Sheik!" said Demon-eye: "but there are three others."

"What will kill one will kill four," said Ali.

"And that is true, O my lord," said Demon-eye, "but then there are the panthers! O Sheik, look at these stripes upon my back. If one lion died, would here be still any skin remaining? If more lions died, how long would the Jew be alive? My head is not so beautiful as that of Rachel's daughter, but it is as useful to me; and, Inshallah, I mean to keep it. Besides, O Sheik!" and here his brutal face softened, "I love my lions, and Nasser is a king of lions, and he knows me. You Arabs love your horses."

A chord in the Arab's bosom vibrated in unison to the feeling in the breast of the Jew, and called up reminiscences, as it were the flash of light upon a picture; he was for a moment absent, and then his eyes beamed mildly on the degraded Jew, on whom he had previously looked with disgust. "God is great!" said Ali. "But where is this to take place, for I must find other means?"

"There is an old fondak," said Demon-eye, "about three hundred yards from the Rahamna gate; it is now seldom used, except when a cafila of black slaves comes in."

The Arab's face brightened. "It has a gate studded with iron, half open," said Ali hastily; "there is a mulberry-tree in the open space in front, and you can just see the top of the Kitibea above the houses. There is a water fountain under the mulberry-tree."

"You know it, O Sheik!" said Ain ed Djin. "But I hope the Rabbi's daughter will not be obstinate; better be a Moslem than eaten by a lion. I have seen these things before, but it never came to blood, for none can look on the face of a lion, with his eyes fixed on them, and no bars between, and not tremble and submit. I will delay to the last, to-morrow afternoon."

Ali had been ruminating, and heard little more than the end of this speech.

"O woman!" he said to Rachel, with a countenance which gave assurance to his words; "be of good cheer, God is merciful, your daughter is safe!"

The building above mentioned, and which was the same visited by Ali on his entrance into the town, related in a former chapter, was the arena chosen for the forthcoming ordeal. Around the centre court a massive colonnade, connected by Gothic arches, supported a roofed gallery, running above the building below; the aisles, formed by the pillars, had originally been divided into small arched rooms, intended for shops for merchants; most of these were now in ruins. The two ends were open, and at the end opposite the gateway, a double row of columns formed a deep recess under the gallery. The court-yard, long neglected, was overgrown here and there with brushwood and brambles. To this place, on the following day, Ain ed Djin removed his favourite Nasser; his heavy cage was placed upon a low truck, and dragged by a number of Jews pressed into the service. Unaccustomed to this mode of conveyance, and half famished, the lion made the crowd tremble with tremendous roars. He was at length safely lodged in a corner of the court-yard near the gate, and a cord fastened to the sliding door of the cage was carried to the gallery above.

It was late in the afternoon when the Sultan's cortege arrived: this was a signal for the crowd to disperse, their movements being accelerated by the sticks of the guards, and only a limited number of the more respectable people were admitted.

Azora in the meantime had been brought to the place in a covered litter in a state of mind impossible to describe, helpless, hopeless, wishing for death to relieve her from her misery. Passing through a crowded part of the bazaars, a ray of hope seemed to gleam upon her, as she heard a voice call out, " Is the black horse ready? " and the reply, " All is safe." It was an assurance that her friends were watchful; but nothing else occurred until she reached her destination.

A canopied seat had been prepared for the Sultan over the gateway within, and here he took his place surrounded by his officers and guards, while Azora was conducted to the end of the court-yard, and left standing in the recess under the colonnade. As the attendants left her, one of them loitered a minute and whispered, " Fear not, the lion shall not hurt you ! " an assurance which could not affect her conviction that nothing short of a miracle could save her if the lion was let loose, and this attempt to raise in her heart a hope impossible of realization was only an aggravation of her sufferings.

One of the scribes in the Sultan's gallery now rose, and in a monotonous voice, as if repeating a lesson, said, " O woman, thou who hast apostatized from the faith of Islam, which thou didst acknowledge, art thou ready to submit to the mercy of our lord the Khalifa, and make the profession, ' There is no God but God, and Mohammed is the Prophet of God?' Behold the

lion is ready to be let loose to destroy the unbeliever."
Here the deep, thundrous growling of the impatient
animal came from the cage, to add emphasis to the ex-
hortation of the Taleb.

The Sultan watched Azora eagerly to detect any
sign of her wavering and appealing to his protection,
but no indication of any change in her resolve met his
eye. She stood absorbed, her hands clasped before
her, and her eyes fixed on the ground. Suddenly
rousing herself as she heard the blasphemy imputed
to her, the spirit of the martyr became strong within
her, she stood erect in her enthusiasm, and a halo of
glory seemed visibly to surround her, as looking up
with one hand aloft and the other pressed to her
bosom, she exclaimed, —

"The Lord he is the God! The Lord he is the
God!"

"Let loose the lion!" said the Sultan; and the
door of the den was drawn up.

There was a dead silence. The lion first put his
huge head cautiously forward, and looked about, but
seeming ashamed of his fear he stepped boldly out and
walked majestically to the middle of the space; here
shaking out his mane to double its volume, he stood
still,—a magnificent monster; then he looked slowly
all round until his deadly eyes rested on the fragile
girl. All held their breath, while the blood ran cold
to every man's heart at this fearful sight.

Poor Azora, though prepared for the worst, seeing
herself almost within the grasp of this powerful and

merciless brute, now frowning fiercely upon her, shook
with a pang of terror, which the bravest man must
have felt in her position. It could not shake her
resolve of dying for her faith, but she mentally prayed
to that God who had delivered the prophet from the
lions, to aid her in her extremity. The lion at first
appeared surprised at being offered a prey, to whose
species he had been so long subject. He stood glaring
on the unfortunate girl and lashing his sides with his
tail, when his instinct suggesting to him that some
cunning was necessary to secure his victim, he walked
away, apparently regardless of her presence, until hid
from her by one of the large columns among the ruins,
when, taking advantage of its concealment, he turned
short round, and, creeping a few paces, uttered a tremendous roar, and sprang with a terrific bound towards his intended victim. A cry of horror burst
involuntarily from all who witnessed this inhuman
scene!

Azora's nature was no longer able to bear up
against the horrors of her situation; drawing her
hands convulsively to her bosom, her eyes distended,
and shrinking instinctively from his fatal spring she
sunk senseless and fainting to the earth. It was the
work of a moment; but before the lion reached her a
double shot had sent two balls through his body, and
the noble animal rolled over within five yards of her,
pierced to the heart, and in the agonies of death. A
natural feeling of relief came over the spectators notwithstanding their fanaticism, and they were probably

not displeased at the change of victims ; but the Sultan could not contain his rage at this unexpected and daring interposition.

"Seize the traitor!" he shouted. "Five hundred gold pieces for the man who fired the shot!"

And the crowd poured in at the gate, some to search for the offender, and some to look at the dying lion.

Among these was poor Ain ed Djin, who sat down and took the enormous head of his pet on his knees till it had ceased to breathe. He made a shrewd guess at the author of his death, but though he loved the lion, his attachment to his race was paramount, and there was no danger of his betraying him.

Azora, as soon as she was restored, was sent back in the litter in which she came. The Sultan was convinced that his experiment was a complete failure, and, not prepared to carry further so illegal a mode of procedure, resolved to hand her over to the sentence of the law.

The parties searching the courtyard were attracted by a cloud of smoke resting on one of the thickets, and on searching the spot they discovered the well ; and near its mouth they found a double gun, its butt on the ground, and the barrel resting on a forked stick planted in the earth, with a string attached to the triggers, and passing out into the courtyard. "El Aarb" (an Arab) passed from mouth to mouth, for they alone use double guns. A man now descended the well, but reported no egress, a mass of rock block-

ing up the passage into the underground canal. All
these circumstances went to prove that the animal had
been killed by a spring gun. This was reported to
the Sultan as the fact, with which he was fain to be
satisfied for the present. There was one in attendance, however, who was not so easily satisfied about
the catastrophe of the lion's death as the Sultan; this
was Abdslem: he and Hassan had not been so long
plotting together without being acquainted with each
other's secrets, and it was perfectly plain to him that
the passage to the well had been made use of for
bringing about the termination to the scene they had
just witnessed. He knew of Hassan's repentance,
and who but he was interested in saving Azora, and
who else was acquainted with the passage? He had no
doubt in his mind but that Hassan was the culprit,
and his belief was confirmed on looking round and
finding that he was absent. They had latterly avoided
each other, but Abdslem's cupidity was excited by the
offered reward of the Sultan; and while all were searching or busy on the spot, he quitted the fondak alone,
and made his way to the town gate with the intention of intercepting Hassan at the pit outside the
walls.

Hassan, who had been horrified at the ordeal he
heard was preparing for Azora, had remained at home,
but at length unable to restrain his anxiety with
respect to the success of Ali's project for her deliverance, he had wandered away outside the town; and
soon after arriving near the fosse he heard the report

of the Arab's gun, and he retired and sat down under
a tree to wait for him. A quarter of an hour had
passed and Ali came not, but presently hearing some
one approach he turned round, and saw it was his
former ally Abdslem; this alarmed Hassan on Ali's
account, but before he could decide on the mode of
getting rid of him, Abdslem addressed him,—

"We have travelled that road before together."

"What road, O unwelcome one?" said Hassan.

"Underground," said Abdslem, jeeringly.

"Where you will soon be, O evil-eyed one, if
you do not go whence you came. I know not what
you talk of."

"How should you, O poor man?" said Abdslem;
"you know nothing of the wonderful case in the
fondak? You cannot shoot lions; we do not know the
well; and here you are taken in the fact?"

Hassan's eye was beginning to glow.

"Wilt thou not go thy ways, O accursed one? I
want not thy company."

"I know it, O darweesh!" said Abdslem, "but
I want yours. In the name of the Sultan I summon
you. Follow me."

"Ha! ha! the Sultan! O son of a black father,
go! Return—I follow not a slave."

Abdslem derived courage from the knowledge that
if he killed Hassan, he would not only be justified
but rewarded. He therefore advanced upon him,
saying,—

"Come you must; it is the Sultan's command."

Hassan had sprung to his feet, Abdslem rushed upon him, and a struggle ensued; Abdslem was the stronger man, and coming prepared, his dagger was first in his hand, and after a short struggle both came to the ground, Hassan under.

"Will you surrender?" said Abdslem, holding down Hassan's dagger hand, while he raised his own to strike.

"Never!" grinned Hassan, glaring upon him and catching his uplifted arm.

Abdslem's whole attention was engaged in the struggle, and he was thus prevented from noticing the presence of Ali el Bezz, who during this time had emerged from the pit and approached them. But what was his dismay on hearing a voice repeat the warning of the Duquela gate, "Beware the Falcon's swoop!" and looking up terror-struck, he met the stern glance of his former prisoner, who stood over him, and before he could recover from his surprise Ali's attaghan was buried in his throat.

As Abdslem fell, Hassan arose.

"May you be rewarded, O my friend!" he said. "The slave was too strong for me; but Azora—is she saved?"

"Saved!" said Ali; "the lion is dead, and the Sultan's beard is defiled."

"And suppose the pan had flashed," said Hassan, with a shudder.

"Both shots would not have failed; the worst is, I have lost an old friend, for I was forced to leave my good gun, to deceive the Sultan's slipper-hunters."

"But," said Hassan, " why did you delay, they will find the well, and you will be pursued?"

"Dost thou see Sheik Ali's ears growing," he said, " that I should lock the door and give my enemy the key? Before I took my station I had filled up the passage with the exception of space for me to pass, and a big rock was loosened ready to shut, that, so I waited when all was done to see if they intended to open the way. But, no! one came down—I could have touched him through the crevices, and he shouts, 'There is no passage; the rocks of creation are here; it is a trap gun.' Oh, that Moslems should be such fools; may their houses be desolate!"

"God is wonderful," said Hassan, "and this lying witness, is he not accursed? But stop! if I go now, and retract my perjury, there will be no witness against her."

" I see not, O friend, how that can help her, they have the writing sworn. But what think you the Sultan cares for your witness? his will is law."

"No! he dare not," said Hassan, " the witnesses must be present, or her blood will be on the people."

"Trust it not; the eagle wants no witness against the dove; but what shall we do with this?" said Ali, pointing to the body.

"Cast him into the pit," said Hassan, " he may be wanted, and I can find him; he knew the road before, this is the last time he will use it; " and taking him between them they swung him over the side, and the body went crashing through the boughs to the bottom of the pit.

It was now getting late, and Ali promising to meet Hassan at his house after dark, they parted.

CHAPTER XIV.

RETRIBUTION.

ASSAN returned to his home, a prey to re-morse. Azora had escaped this time, but the final scene awaited her. Men's motives are of a mixed nature, and difficult to analyse. I do not assume that he was solely moved by the stings of conscience, or that he had any great horror of perjury in the abstract; but, however the customs of a country may modify the modes of expressing the feelings, and of acting under their guidance, there is no doubt that he entertained for Azora a pure and ardent love. Prompted by his false friend and urged on by his passion, he had adopted the only course which appeared to him capable of compassing his end, without calculating the obstacles which might arise, and which he could not foresee, and when the full view of the consequences of his act was forced upon him he was appalled. Not only to lose one he loved so deeply, but to feel that he, who would willingly have sacrificed his life for her, had been the means of bringing her to an awful and cruel death; it was more than his mind could bear. Azora's forgiveness was no relief to him in the bitterness of his grief; the more he felt the innocence and purity of her nature, the deeper he felt the enormity of his own guilt, in devoting such an angel to destruction; reproaches, even curses, he could have borne, her gentleness and forgiveness were intolerable.

To-night, as he entered his dwelling, he felt a gloomy foreboding, as if some heavy retribution were hanging over him. His little sister,—a bright creature with hazel eyes and a laughing face,—ran to meet him. The care of this child had devolved upon him since the death of his parents, and she was now coming to the age when her playful and affectionate manners began to reward him for his care and protection; his little darling sprang joyfully into his arms, and kissed his cold lips; he clasped her to his breast, and felt a transient feeling of relief.

"Oh, how happy we might have been," he said, half aloud,—"lost!—lost!" and the conviction of his misery overpowered every other sensation. He smoothed back the silken tresses from her fair forehead, and gazed on her sweet face, talking almost involuntarily. "Once I was like you,—innocent,—but now—"

"Are you ill, brother dear?" said the child, putting its arms round his neck. "Brother, don't play with me, but brother is pale,—not well, and I don't want to play. If you are sick, I shall cry all night."

"No, love," said Hassan, shrinking from her innocent scrutiny, "I am not sick, but very tired; and now it is time for you to go to bed; is it not late?"

The child allowed itself to be put to bed quietly,

in the adjoining room, the door of which was left ajar,
that Hassan might hear if she wanted anything during
the night. He was now alone, he tried in vain to
make light of the weight, and cast off the gloom
which oppressed his spirits, and he sat with his hands
pressed to his forehead harrowed with inward suffering; presently a ghastly smile overspread his features,
as a horrible thought presented itself to his mind, and
he drew his dagger with a convulsive start. "Thus,
then, I can escape this load of misery," said he, gazing
at its keen tapering point. "Why should man live
and suffer with such an antidote as this?—But stop!
will not this add another crime to my account? And
I may yet be of service to Azora. O Azora, Azora!
what woe has not your love brought upon me? And
alas! upon you. And who, when I am gone, will take
care of this sweet child?" As these thoughts succeeded each other, his resolution gradually gave way,
and with a shudder he hurled the weapon of death to
the other end of the room. A shrill, prolonged scream
of infant agony instantly burst on his ears; and as he
sprang aghast to the spot, his little sister fell writhing
at his feet transfixed by the deadly steel. The child
had been impressed with the idea that her brother
was ill; and when she heard him talking to himself,
and so uneasy, with child-like curiosity she crept
quietly from her bed, and had just entered the half-
open door, when she was struck by the fatal dagger,
and fell deluged in blood.

Hassan remained fixed to the spot, paralysed with

horror, his eyes starting from their sockets, his mouth
open, his hands clenched, a petrified image of despair.
For some minutes he seemed not to breathe; presently
he dropped on his knees, he raised the child's head,
and pressed his lips to hers; the blood oozed from the
pressure and ran a crimson stream down her neck,
staining her silken hair; his lips were damp with her
blood; his brain, already shaken, could no longer bear
up against the shock, gasping for breath he fell senseless on the floor. Gradually, after some time, sensation
returned, but when it did, his reason had left him.
He sat up, and looked round the room with a vacant
stare, till his eye rested on the body of the child; this
recalled the lost thread of his thoughts; snatching the
dagger from the wound, he sprang to his feet with
a heart-freezing yell, as he brandished it aloft.

"Ha! ha! ha! fiends, are ye content? Nó! I
come! I come! Shower down upon me the burning
rafters of hell!—O Azora, you are avenged! God, how
my heart burns, it is like a ball of fire in my bosom,
and this red-tempered steel will fuse, ere it pierce it.
Lo, I come!"

His hand was already raised to accomplish his
purpose, when Ali, who had just entered, rushed forward and wrenched the dagger from his grasp, in
doing which he stumbled against the child.

"Hassan! what mean you? Whose work is this?
Are you mad?

Hassan sprang frantically forward—

"Mad, did you say?" he yelled; "mad! aye,

mad! mad! mad!" and he dashed himself on the earth and howled hideously in a paroxysm of fury. Ali perceived at once that his reason had given way, and supposed that he had destroyed his sister in the blindness of his rage. Leaving him to exhaust himself where he lay, Ali removed the body to the adjoining room, and having washed away the stains from the ,floor, he sat down to consider the best course to adopt to prevent harm to Hassan or himself on account of the crime of the former. He was fearful of exciting Hassan by asking an explanation; but from this he was saved by Hassan himself, who now rose slowly from the ground, and looked with a long searching glance round the room. His appearance was frightful; his turban had fallen off, exposing his shaven head; his pallid face, stained with blood, contrasted with his black moustaches and glittering eyes; the veins in his neck and temples were swollen to bursting,—his whole face distorted. The stout heart of the Arab could not divest him of a superstitious misgiving, as he looked on the figure of his friend; he, lately so calm, now the prey of insanity.

Hassan pressed his hands to his eyes, to try and realise the past, and then stood wreathing and winding his fingers together.

"Horrid dream! what art thou?" he said, in a ,hollow voice, and turning to Ali, "O Moslem, let me remember; yes, she is safe. O Azora, thou art safe! Methought I returned home—home? My destiny was darkened—clouds and darkness were over me. Me-

thought my little darling flew into my arms—I kissed
her. Ha! again! is it blood? No! no! I dream
still! I laid her in her bed—she sleeps—no noise—
she sleeps! I laid my burning brow on the table; I
thought it would have burnt into it. When I lifted
my eyes, Iblis stood before me. My dagger was in
my hand. 'Strike!' he said." Here Hassan twisted
his hands more eagerly, and his whole frame was trembling. "The keen blade glittered like a lambent
moonbeam; I sprang to my feet. Satan avaunt! I
cast it from me. Ha! what do I hear? the demoniac
laugh of the retreating fiend, and the agonized cry of
my murdered child. There she is, see, at my feet—
bleeding—dead!"

Large drops followed one another down the brow
and face of Hassan, but he was deadly calm, and
seemed to repeat the words from memory, but to have
no feeling of their meaning.

Ali, finding he did not relapse, took advantage of
the pause to soothe his spirits and divert his thoughts—
it was needless. His memory just recollected the bare
outline of the scene, but without consciousness, and he
did not even ask for his sister.

"God has smitten the oppressors of the innocent,"
muttered Ali, while Hassan fell into an apathetic
stupor; reaction of the violent emotions which had so
shaken him. Ali had now to consider what was best
to be done; Hassan could no further co-operate with
him, and for him to present himself to the authorities
under any circumstances would ensure his destruction.

Ali wrote on a piece of paper, "Hassan Ibn Ibrahim, possessed with an evil spirit, slew his sister," and after removing Hassan's dagger, and everything he might make use of to injure himself, he took the child's body, and, during the night, left it with the billet at the gate of the Cadi, knowing that, when discovered in the morning, inquiry would be made, the truth be apparent, and the affair hushed up.

CHAPTER XV.

THE PLEDGE REDEEMED.

AS soon as they arrived at the cultivated districts, which they did by rapid marches, the Arabs spread themselves over the country, plundering in all directions. For this purpose they dispersed by tribes, the whole body uniting for the night at a rendezvous previously fixed upon. The peasants fled everywhere on their approach, securing what property they had time to remove, into the towns and walled villages. These, the Arabs being all horsemen, left unmolested. They carried off all the grain that could be discovered, and even reaped what was on the ground, compelling the peasants to assist in threshing it out; they also gathered the dates from the trees. Their plunder was loaded on camels and mules, seized on their route. Wherever they bivouacked, their horses were picketed in the standing corn, and very soon changed their appearance from the bony, game-looking animals that they were at starting, to rounded, sleek chargers. The cultivated tracts they passed over were left as if a swarm of locusts had swept over the land. After issuing the necessary orders to the Sheiks left in command, and directing their course on the province of Rahamna, Sheik Hamed selected five hundred of his best horsemen, and started by forced marches for Marocco, having received an urgent message from Ali that no time was to be lost if he wished to be assured of redeeming his word. About fifty miles south of the city, the Chief knew that he would find a tribe of Arabs, who, although settled in the province, kept up a friendly intercourse with the original desert stock. From the douar of this tribe, he could march by a straight course much faster than any messenger who might be on his way to give notice of their approach; and by avoiding any molestation of the peasants on the march, through a sparsely populated and thickly-wooded country, very little alarm would be excited. It was the day before the execution that the Chief arrived at this place, called Ras el Ain, early in the morning. He did not inform his hosts of the object of his visit, but as rumours of the irruption of the tribes had reached even to Marocco, they were supposed to be a reconnoitring party. After resting all day, hospitably entertained by the tribe, the Chief called to horse at sunset, and made a night march of forty miles, stopping in the woods, within ten miles of the town, where were some springs, among masses of rock. The forest trees were high, and interspersed with glades; but in a place so utterly unfrequented, that any number of horsemen might have been easily concealed. By travelling single file from this spot, the band could debouch on the plain within two miles of the gates of the town. Yusuf was sent on at once from here, to apprise Rachel of the approaching

succour, as, whether the plans of the Chief succeeded
or failed, it would not be safe for either of them to
remain within the Sultan's power; they were therefore
to repair to this place, where one hundred horsemen
would be left in reserve. Yusuf was also to communicate with Ali, who was waiting impatiently for tidings
of the Chief. In case of his failing to arrive, Ali would
certainly have attempted the rescue, with his small
band; but then there was the danger of being pursued
by the Moors, who would have been encouraged by the
weakness of his numbers, whereas, against a larger
force, they would not venture to leave the protection of
their walls, until after tedious preparation and the col-
lection of an army.

The day appointed for the accomplishing of the
martyrdom of Azora had arrived. The Sultan was
sitting in the M'Shouar, attended by his guards, while
on carpets near him sat the Wezeer and scribes,—one
of these was preparing the warrant of execution for the
Sultan's seal. The order set forth that she was to be
taken outside the gates, at the hour of mid-day prayer,
and to be burnt alive at the stake as an apostate from
the faith of Islam. The audience-hall, which was supported by pillars, opened in front on a large public
place, to which the people had access, and here a considerable crowd was collected, attracted by the novelty
of the case. As a mob, they were eager for the excitement of an execution; this, in the present instance,
was enhanced by their fanaticism, and they looked
forward to the burning of an infidel with peculiar

gratification. The crowd, however, maintained a respectful distance, and any breach of order brought on them an indiscriminate shower of blows from the sticks of the black soldiers. Those who came on business of importance, or had causes to be heard, were allowed to enter the hall, one at a time. While the preliminaries of this judicial murder were being effected, there was a movement among the crowd, and a man, in a hooded burnoose, walked slowly into the audience-hall; he held a staff in his hand, and from his wrist hung, by a thong, a mace headed by an iron ball, studded with spikes, such as is often carried by mendicant fakeers.

"What is his business?" said the Sultan, as he stood before him.

The stranger allowed the hood of his cloak to fall from his head, and discovered the pale, wild features of Hassan. He fixed his eyes, glittering with the fire of insanity, on the Sultan.

"Dost thou know me?" said he, slowly, whilst all present trembled for his life, "I am Hassan Ibn Ibrahim: but where is my father? He died in the tyrant's prison. Where is my father's house? I—I alone, remain, and I care not how soon you send me to their graves: but first I have an errand. Hear, O Moslemin!" he said, raising his voice, "I come here to confess my perjury. That woman, that child of God, that you are here assembled to murder, is innocent—I (may I be accursed!) accused her falsely. I retract—I demand her freedom. Let the law judge my crime."

Maniacs are looked upon by the Moors with reverential awe, and allowed to roam at large. They are believed to be possessed by spirits, by whose inspiration they speak. The Sultan quailed under the gaze of the madman; but, though boiling with rage at being thus thwarted in his sanguinary purpose, he controlled himself; and, more to justify himself to the people, than supposing the maniac could understand him, he said, mildly,—

"It is too late; your accusation was written and sworn : and supposing you were guilty of perjury, as you say, but which is to be doubted, yet the other witness maintaining his word, your present falsehood is useless."

The maniac's features worked wildly, and his eyes flashed, while the Sultan was speaking. The mildness of his reception had inspired him with greater boldness.

"Ha! ha! ha!" he yelled. "Iblis whispered me this, and told me to come prepared."

He threw open his cloak, and produced a bundle, enveloped in the embroidered scarf lately given by the Sultan to Abdslem.

"Dost thou know that scarf?" he continued, "did it not belong to the false witness? And if he does not admit himself a perjured slave and confess the innocence of Azora, his accursed tongue will never again say that she is guilty.—Behold!" and unrolling the scarf with a jerk, the ghastly head of Abdslem fell on the Sultan's carpet.

The eyes of the maniac literally blazed with rapture,

on beholding the effect he had produced, he ground his teeth, and the foam flew from his mouth.

"There!—there!" he shouted, rushing towards the Sultan, then suddenly stopping and pointing to it with his staff—"ask him—behold your witness—does he accuse her? then I must answer for him," said he, raising his voice to the highest pitch. "I swear that she is innocent, and every fiend in hell re-echoes, 'She is innocent!'"

The Sultan, though restrained by superstition, hardly considered himself safe in such close proximity to the madman, yet did not wish to evince his alarm, but his hand went mechanically into his vest for a pistol or dagger. This movement did not escape the eye of the maniac—he yelled a hideous laugh, that thrilled the hearts of his hearers.

"Ha! he fears me, he is a Sultan—but guilt always fears. You slew my father, why should you not fear me? My sister!"

His brain scethed as the horrid vision of her death flashed on his broken intellect, and he gazed an instant at his clenched hands.

"Yes! her blood is upon them."

The vision passed as it came, and he spoke again in calm tones as of reason.

"I warn you that you are in danger; I devote you to human vengeance and divine wrath! For the last time I demand Azora's liberation."

The Sultan's patience was at length exhausted,

"Seize him, and off with his head!" he thundered springing up.

Frenzy again blazed in the eye of Hassan : " Stop !" he shouted, as he dropped on his knee; "and may the curse of Mohammed and the Seven Sleepers cleave to the man that lays a hand on me !" then, springing to his feet, and swinging his mace round his head, he uttered a prolonged yell of triumph, and rushed through the crowd that recoiled terror-struck to open him a passage, and his shouts of vengeance rang in their ears until they died away in the distance.

This incident was not calculated to influence the Sultan's decision, but rather to increase his irritation against his victim. It would hardly have altered his resolve had the two witnesses come, like Judas, and said, "We have sinned, in that we have betrayed the innocent blood." But one being dead, and the other a madman, it left the case exactly as it stood.

At midday the fatal procession left the town by the Rahamna gate. First walked the Cadi and his secretaries, a green banner being carried before him : then followed the condemned martyr, in a long linen veil, surrounded by some thirty or forty guards, on foot and on horseback. Then came the executioners with torches, ropes, and long knives, a large crowd of horse and foot from the town followed. As they left the gate, they raised the usual chaunt, " La Illaw Il Allah, Mohammed er rasool Allaw." This was taken up by the crowd, and the poor girl's heart sunk within her;

she had not lost all hope, as she had received intimations, not very clear, that an attempt would be made to deliver her, and she started as she heard the following words, from two men in the crowd, just outside the guards, " *Is the black horse saddled?* " and the reply, "*Ay, Inshallah! and will win.*" She remembered the signal of her escape from the lion, and she hoped almost against hope, but in any case she was prepared to meet her God.

"Where is the race?" said Abd el Aziz, who was one of the guards, deceived by the stranger's speech.

"The other side of the town, O Kaïd!" said the stranger; "we had a wager on our horses, but followed this crowd, to see the execution, but my heart sickens at the thought of it—a woman too!"

"I don't like it myself," said Abd el Aziz, "but I am a slave of the Sultan, his word must stand. If it had been a man—I know this one, and the infidel is beautiful. May I not be unmanned and shame my beard—you are not a Marokshi."

"No! I am from Rif," said the horseman.

"Rif!" said Abd el Aziz, "you are all pirates in Rif—and you pretend to be soft-hearted."

"There are pirates in Rif, O Kaïd, and there are thieves in Marocco, but there are mountaineers in Rif, who never saw the sea. I heard that the witnesses against this infidel had retracted."

"How could that be?" said Abd el Aziz; "Hassan, who is possessed with a devil, came to the M'Shouar and brought his friend's head under his arm to confirm him; but as one could not speak, and the devil spoke in the other, the Sultan was only more savage; he would have killed Hassan, had it pleased God, but who would touch a Majnoon?"

"Inshallah!" said the stranger, "I cannot stand this burning, and you say she is beautiful." Then raising his voice, he said, "*The black horse is waiting. If she is innocent, God will send her deliverance—Peace.*"

"Inshallah!" repeated Abd el Aziz, "when the mountain comes to our lord Mohammed;" and our friend Ali, dressed as a Moor, turned back with his companion, and galloped across the plain to a date-grove, where he had collected his followers; they were partly screened from observation, but as they were all dressed as Moors, any passers-by supposed them to be a troop of the Sultan's soldiers on some duty, more especially as they guarded a woman's litter carried between two stout mules. One of the party was stationed in the top of a date-tree which overlooked the plain, and reported every thing that took place; he could see the preparations at the place of execution, and give early notice of any movement in the distance.

On a slight rising ground, about half a mile from the gates, the pile of wood had been raised. It was about eight feet high, built up around a stake fixed in the ground. The wood being a species of cedar was very inflammable, and to make it more so a quantity of pitch and turpentine had been added to it. A little apart, under the shade of a large tree, carpets had been spread for the Cadi and his party; here he took his seat, attended by the horsemen, while the foot-soldiers kept clear the space around the pile. It would be a slander on the better classes of the Moors, to suppose that they felt any of the pleasure of inquisitors, in witnessing, or being actors in, a tragedy like the present, on the contrary they were not only impressed with its impolicy, but shocked by its inhumanity and cruelty. Cases had occurred in which young Jews, in a fit of temporary irritation, arising out of family quarrels, had really apostatized, but had been allowed on proper representations made, accompanied by the judicious expenditure of money, to return to their own people; and so might Azora, but for the curse of beauty.

The Jews, for the most part, remained within doors, mourning for their sister, and bewailing the captivity of their people; but some few had gone out of the gate, afraid to approach, but standing afar off to see the end of the martyr to their faith.

Azora was first taken before the Cadi, and a crier called out the names of the witnesses, her accusers, but no one answered; after a pause, the names were again called, and again a third time without answer. The Cadi then produced his records, and the sworn deposition was read out. After this he read out the warrant of the Sultan for her execution. The old man's voice trembled, and he looked wistfully in Azora's face in hopes of seeing some sign of her recantation. She was deadly pale, but as a sheep before her shearers, she was dumb, and they led her away to be burnt. At the pile her veil was taken off, and her face was as the face of an angel. With the exception of the brutified executioners, there were very few, even to the rough soldiers, who were not in tears.

Sheik Ali in the meantime was in a state of the most intense anxiety, on account of the delay of the Chief. As soon as he arrived at the ambush, he never took his eyes from the look-out, who sat among the feathery fronds of the date-tree, and reported what he saw in broken sentences.

"What seest thou, O brother?" said Ali.

"Nothing, O Sheik! The procession passes on."

"And in the distance?—your eyes were wont to be good," said Ali.

"Nothing, O Sheik! The plain is white;—the procession has arrived;—the green flag of Islam is planted near a tree.—Two vultures have risen from the woods, on the south of the plain.—The woman is being taken towards the pile of wood."

"Mount!" said Ali, becoming desperate, and every man was in his saddle.

"A jackal has broken from the wood," resumed the scout, "it crosses the plain—looking back.—Now I think I see our people;—they emerge from the woods; —they are forming outside;—a body is left in reserve; —I see the Chief at the head of his band! Lo! they come!"

And the next minute he had slid to the ground.

Azora stood on the pile, in relief against the clear sky; one of the executioners was preparing the ropes to attach her to the stake, while the other stood by with the torch awaiting the order from the Cadi to fire the pile. Suddenly there was a movement of alarm among the crowd, and Azora's eye brightened, as, looking across the plain in the direction in which they swayed, she saw a cloud of dust approaching from the south; immediately afterwards a cry was raised, "El Aarb! El Aarb! Fly! fly! The Arabs! the Arabs!" and in a few minutes the whole crowd was flying across the plain which separated them from the town, and streaming towards the gates like frightened cattle. Down came the dark mass of cavalry charging at full speed; the earth shook, and from three hundred voices rose above the noise and screams of the crowd the wild shout, "Allaw ho Ackbar!" Onward came the Arabs, in every variety of costume, turbans, and burnooses, from the marauding expedition, put over their blue shirts; their guns poised, they swept over the comparatively abandoned space, separating as they passed the pile; they trampled on or struck down the affrighted stragglers, and wheeling, brought up beyond. The Chief, with Sheik Ayoub, were in the centre of the charge, and checking their speed as they came up, Ayoub sprang from his saddle to the top of the pile, and cutting with his attaghan the cords with which he had already begun to bind his victim, he dashed the executioner to the earth; the dogged villain, enraged at losing his prey, was up the next minute, and climbing the wood pile on the other side, dagger in hand to rush on Azora, when he

o

was confronted by the glaring eye of Hassan the maniac, who with one blow of his mace shattered his skull, and hurled him, this time, lifeless to the ground. In the meantime, the other executioner, inspired by the hate of fanaticism, before he attempted to escape, threw his torch into the prepared pile, which was instantly in a blaze; he was cut down and trampled under foot; but there was no time to be lost, and Azora, half fainting, was lowered down and placed in the litter, which had been sent forward by Ali.

Ali, while this had been going on, had not been idle; emerging from the grove, with a plume of black ostrich-feathers carried on a spear, to distinguish him to his tribesmen, he galloped down and surrounded the party of cavalry round the Cadi. Being dressed as Moors, these at first supposed they were friends come to their assistance, until they found themselves each with a double-barrel at his breast, and before they could recover from their surprise, they were all disarmed, and their horses hobbled; the Cadi and his scribes wondering whether it was written that their throats were to be cut by the Arabs.

"Resistance is useless," said Ali to the soldiers.

"You have seen me before, O my lord the Cadi!" and Al Maimon's face was as white as his beard at finding himself in the power of one who was looked on as an afreet, and who had so often escaped from his sentences.

"Ali el Bezz!" he ejaculated, "O Sheik! I know you. God is merciful—I am an old man—I never wronged you—I give sentence according to law— but revenge is yours! Let me say the Fetha, and take my life—if it is written."

" Truly, O Al Maimon, you deserve to die, as an unjust judge. Do you not pervert the holy Koran for your purposes? Do you not take bribes to rob God's children, the widow and orphan? and are you not now here to shed innocent blood? But your victim is safe, and we have taught you the difference between Moorish law and Arab justice. I will not have your blood on my hands, when your grey beard will so soon be burning in Djehennem. You will presently be free. Show mercy, as you have received it. And tell your Sultan we laugh at his beard."

" O Sheik!" said Abd el Aziz, " the black horse has won the race."

Their attention was now attracted by a succession of yells from the burning pyre: " Woe unto you, Moslim! Woe unto you, murderers! Woe! woe! Slay, O Sheik! cut them down! spare none! The Prophet's curse on them! Woe! woe!" And they beheld Hassan the maniac on the summit of the pile, now wrapped in flames, with his arms wildly waving, and shouting his curses. The Chief would have saved him, but Hassan, unable to distinguish friend from foe, warned them off: "Woe unto you, murderers; you shall not take me alive! Death to the slave who approaches! Slay, O Ali!"—Here the smoke and flame rolled upward, and choked his utterance, and his voice broke into gurgling and spasmodic screams, as the fire wrapped him round, and his clothes and hair were fiercely ablaze. On the same spot where the vision of the Hebrew maiden had just before appeared against the sky, now stood forth the burning and appalling form of her accuser. He stood erect, one blackened arm pointing towards the band, the other wound round the glowing stake, a figure of horror. With a dying effort, as the wind blew the smoke from his face, he sent up a last sad cry, " O Azora! Azora! saved! saved! Allaw ho Ackbar! " and sank devoured in the flaming pyre.

The crowd had disappeared within the town gates, with the exception of some dozen maimed, who had been ridden down by the Arabs' charge. Leaving the Cadi and his party at liberty, the whole band resumed their march, escorting the litter by the way they came. The sun shone on the vacant plain, on the black smouldering pile, on the whispering date-groves, and on the mud walls of the town, now manned with excited spectators, who did not, however, venture out, until the band of the Arab Chief, who had so nobly redeemed his Pledge, gradually disappeared behind the distant woods.

FINIS.

LONDON: STRANGEWAYS & WALDEN, PRINTERS,
Castle Street, Leicester Square.